June 29—I wanted Habib to tell me about the wave of arrests that was going on, but I didn't want to tell him about my father. Since he lives a little ways from us, he hadn't witnessed it. I asked, and Habib only grew still; he did not answer. After a while he asked if I had read the Gibran. I shouted that Gibran was of no interest to me just now; I wanted to know about the arrests because a friend of mine had been detained for no reason. He kept silent and looked sorrowfully into my eyes.

"For no reason? Since when does this government need a reason to torture people?"

"Pushes the subject of censorship way beyond the usual YA problems ... to matters of life and death." —*School Library Journal*

"A crystalline window into the many-faceted world of the Middle East."
—*Kirkus reviews*, pointer review

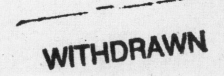

WITHDRAWN

A Hand Full of Stars

by Rafik Schami

translated from the German
by Rika Lesser

PUFFIN BOOKS

PUFFIN BOOKS
Published by the Penguin Group
Penguin Books USA Inc., 375 Hudson Street, New York, New York 10014, U.S.A.
Penguin Books Ltd, 27 Wrights Lane, London W8 5TZ, England
Penguin Books Australia Ltd, Ringwood, Victoria, Australia
Penguin Books Canada Ltd, 10 Alcorn Avenue, Toronto, Ontario, Canada M4V 3B2
Penguin Books (N.Z.) Ltd, 182–190 Wairau Road, Auckland 10, New Zealand

Penguin Books Ltd, Registered Offices: Harmondsworth, Middlesex, England

First published in Germany by Beltz Verlag under the title
Eine Hand voller Sterne, 1987
First published in the United States of America by Dutton Children's Books,
a division of Penguin Books USA Inc., 1990
Published in Puffin Books, 1992

1 3 5 7 9 10 8 6 4 2

LIBRARY OF CONGRESS CATALOGING-IN-PUBLICATION DATA
Schami, Rafik, 1946–
[Hand voller Sterne. English]
A hand full of stars / by Rafik Schami; English translation by Rika Lesser.   p. cm.
Translation of: Eine Hand voller Sterne.
Summary: A teenager who wants to be a journalist in a suppressed
society describes to his diary his daily life in his hometown of Damascus, Syria.
ISBN 0-14-036073-5
[1. Syria—Fiction. 2. Diaries—Fiction.] I. Title.
PZ7.S3337Han 1992   [Fic]—dc20   92-8872

Printed in the United States of America
Set in Aster

to Marie and Therese,
my sisters
R. S

The
First
Year

January 12 — One day my old friend, so dear to me that I call him "Uncle" Salim, said to me: "What a pity I can't write. I have experienced so much that was important. Today I no longer know what has kept me for years from sleeping at night."

"But you know quite a lot, Uncle," I comforted him.

"No, my friend," he said. "Of the landscape, nothing will remain but the mountains, and later only their peaks will be visible, and all of it will sink into the mist. If I had learned to write, I would have the power to preserve the mountains, fields, and valleys, and every single thorn on the stem of a rose. What wonderful people the Chinese are!"

I was surprised Uncle Salim had suddenly landed among the Chinese. When I asked him about it, he explained: "By inventing paper, the Chinese made it possible for the art of reading and writing to be accessible to everyone. From the temples of scholars and the palaces of kings the Chinese brought writing to the streets. They are marvelous."

And so, after tea at Uncle Salim's, I decided to keep a

journal. I forget a lot. I can't even remember the name of the mother of my first girlfriend, Samira. My head is like a sieve.

I want to write every day!

January 21 — Today I helped my father in the bakery. Two of his employees weren't there. So he had to knead and shape the dough himself, and then stand at the oven. I took care of the cash register. As a rule, the customers bring their own shopping bags. Whoever forgets gets his bread wrapped in newspaper.

Early in the morning the shop was peaceful. I read the newspaper, even though my father complained, saying I ought to take care of the bread. But I'm used to his griping, and besides, I know when it's one of his serious requests and when it's just one of his fits of grumbling. I went on reading, and then I saw the little article about journal writing.

"A journal is a rearview mirror." I thought about this for quite a while. Somehow or other it went along with what Uncle Salim had said. (To my shame, I must admit that since I started to keep this journal, I have written no more than one page. I've only been talking about writing.) The article went on in an amusing way, saying that only a few people can keep an honest journal. Others lie, although the worst liar among them still has a mirror later—a distorting mirror, as at a fair, and one can laugh about it. I never lie without good cause. Mostly only because grown-ups don't understand me.

I am fourteen years old, and I swear I want to keep on writing. I have a hiding place for the journal where no one will find it. That's why I can write from my soul.

January 25 — I want to jot down what our quarter in Damascus looks like. My parents have moved three times since I was born, and I no longer know exactly how the previous houses looked. The street we live on now is rather narrow. It is in the eastern part of the city. Near my house is St. Paul's Chapel. Many tourists visit the place from which the apostle Paul took off and went to Europe.

Our houses are built of clay. Several families live in each one, and every building has an interior courtyard, which belongs to all the families; here they come together to talk and laugh and sometimes to quarrel. Mainly the adults keep to the courtyard. The street belongs to the children, the beggars, and to itinerant peddlers. Every house has two stories; the roofs are flat and almost all the same height, so you can walk from one roof to another without any trouble.

I still remember the morning we were sitting on our terrace, eating breakfast, when suddenly a young man peered down from the roof. He wanted to know where the door to the house was. My mother showed him. He leaped onto our terrace and from there ran to the stairs and out into the alley.

My mother was just bringing the teapot from the kitchen when two policemen suddenly appeared.

"Have you seen a young Palestinian?" one of them asked.

"A Palestinian? No! Have you no shame, forcing your way into our house! There are women and children here!" my mother cried out.

The policeman apologized, and both of them turned to go. My mother poured tea and went on eating her breakfast as if nothing had happened. Her behavior astonished me.

In the afternoon I had to ask her, "Why did you lie?"

"The young man looked very worried. He has a mother, and she wouldn't report you if you were running away from the police!"

"And how do you know that? Are you sure?"

"Yes, I'm sure. I'm a mother." She smiled and kissed me on the forehead.

February 10 — I have three friends: Uncle Salim, who is seventy-five years old; Mahmud, who is fifteen; and Josef, who is fourteen, exactly my age.

For most of his life Uncle Salim drove a coach, so he tells great stories about robbers, kings, and fairies. He has seen a lot and has survived several famous robbers and kings and, yes, perhaps fairies as well. Uncle Salim, Mahmud, and I all live in the same house. Josef's house is just opposite ours.

Mahmud and Josef have never been outside Syria. I have. I spent two years in a monastery in Lebanon. My father sent me there to make a priest out of me. Every poor family tries to turn a son into a clergyman, because a priest commands respect and gives the family a good reputation. After two years I gave it up.

The pupils came from various Arab countries, but we were forced to speak French. So each newcomer had to take a crash course in that language, and then, after two months, he was no longer permitted to speak a single word of Arabic. If he did, he was given a small, round piece of wood, with the letter S (which stood for *signal*) on it. He had to hide it on his person and secretly wait for some new victim to foist it off on. If he betrayed himself in any way, the other pupils would know he had the signal and avoid him like a skunk. No, he had to accept it quietly and slink around until someone or other unsuspectingly spoke Arabic in his presence. In this way, we were all educated as little spies. Whoever was last to possess the wooden disk had to eat his supper kneeling.

Having the signal was an odd feeling I will never forget. It seemed very warm in your pocket and gave you power over the others. If you got it early enough in the day, you had a lot of leeway. I showed mercy if my would-be victim was someone I liked. But I'd press it gleefully into the hand of an ass-kisser. After a while, secret gangs formed. I belonged to one made up of five students. We vowed to help one another. You couldn't slip the wooden disk to anyone in the gang, so if one of us had it, the other four basked in security and made full use of the opportunity to speak Arabic.

One of the priests got wind of our gang. He railed against using the signal to turn the pupils against one another. But he was laughed off the teaching staff, and the war of the gangs went on.

Some gangs evolved into commandos; members even took the signal at their own peril when it fell into the hands of a less brave member of their gang. Then they would go searching for a victim. Supper was around six, and it was considered a heroic act to take the thing into your possession with only an hour left. One of these kamikazes, an Egyptian, pressed it into the hand of a teacher when the teacher said in Arabic, at a quarter to six, that he was dying of hunger. The other teachers gazed into his palm, stunned. Then they announced the rule against speaking Arabic didn't apply to them; teachers were not part of the game. And so on this evening the little Egyptian had to eat kneeling. This was the first time the pupils showed respect to anyone who had to do so. We pressed his shoulder as we passed by.

February 26 — Uncle Salim often tells stories about fairies. Today he said they have long been living in Syria. He's spoken with them often. They remain underground, in springs and mountain caves, becoming visible only when they speak.

"And why haven't I ever seen a fairy then?" our neighbor Afifa, who always knows better, interrupted him.

Because you never give anyone a chance to speak, I would have said. But Uncle Salim wasn't unkind in the least. He looked at Afifa thoughtfully. "You are right. I haven't seen any either in forty years. The last one told me that they could not stand automobiles, because fairies speak very softly."

Uncle Salim makes strange claims. He says the fairies have bewitched not only the pyramids but also all the ravines in the mountains. According to Salim, the warm springs in the south are the fairies' subterranean baths.

March 10 — Today we punished a motorist who refused to understand that we don't like it when a car speeds down our narrow alley. Josef lay in wait up on his roof, and when the show-off turned around at the end of the alley and raced back down it, honking, Josef flung a stone at the car. The motorist got out in a rage, but there was no one in sight. He cursed when he saw the dent, then slowly drove out of the alley.

March 20 — Mr. Katib is a terrific teacher. His predecessor taught us to fear and respect language; Mr. Katib teaches us to love it. Earlier we had been told that imagination resided in exaggeration alone, but now Mr. Katib teaches us that fabulous tales transpire in the simple events of our everyday lives. Our previous teacher never let us describe the fragrance of flowers or the flight of swallows. All he ever wanted us to write about were fantastic banquets, birthdays, "experiences." But not a single one of us from impoverished homes has ever experienced an exceptional birthday or a great feast.

I will never forget the pupil who, in my opinion, wrote the best composition. We were supposed to describe a banquet.

Whenever guests show up at our house—and they often appear out of nowhere—my mother shares everything she has with them. My mother always cooks so much, I think she is constantly expecting visitors. When we have guests, we eat with them, and in their honor my father drinks two glasses of *arrack*, to be sure the guests will join him in a drink.

Had I described it truthfully, I would not even have gotten a D on my composition. So I went running to Uncle Salim, because he had taken many rich people to celebrations and parties in his coach. Once there, he would often sneak into the kitchen and eat with the cooks and the house staff. He described exactly what was served and how, the beverages people drank, and everything they talked about. A few pashas and princes (which no longer exist in Syria) came marching into Uncle Salim's stories, but I replaced them with the chief of police and even a judge (no judge has ever seen the inside of our apartment!). I wrote that my mother served them a roasted gazelle, stuffed with almonds, rice, and raisins. And of course I recounted the words of praise the judge uttered about my parents' meal and the *arrack*. It was funny to have only a bit of dry bread in my knapsack during recess but to go on about roast gazelle. None of my schoolmates laughed. They just stared at me with their mouths open. I got a B and listened, just as much a zombie, to the stories of the others, in which bishops, generals, poets, and traders suddenly joined hands in our poverty-stricken dwellings.

Chalil alone did not play along. When it was his turn, he told the story of what had happened when he asked his parents what a banquet was. His mother immediately went into raptures, at the same time bemoaning her bad luck in having married such a poor man as her husband, despite having been courted, when she was young, by many suitors who were richer. Chalil's father became hurt and angry; he said he would have been a rich man long ago had he not been forced to feed her large and voracious family (twelve siblings, father, mother, and grandfather). A colleague of his had a good wife, and on the same salary as his they had built two houses. Then Chalil's mother yelled at his father that her parents always brought a lot with them when they came, and that if he didn't buy *arrack,* he could have scraped together the money for a home long ago. His parents argued a long time. Each of us saw our own families reflected in Chalil's.

Chalil ended his report with the following sentence: "In order to keep them from getting a divorce, I have sworn never again to ask my parents about a banquet!"

The teacher gave him an F. "Theme lacking."

Chalil did not return the next day or any other. Now he works in an auto repair shop.

March 30 — Every day Uncle Salim listens to the news. He crouches in front of his old radio, a tense expression on his face; visitors are not even allowed to cough. He is better informed about what happens in the world than our teachers.

Today, when I came to see him, he was in a cheerful mood. The news was that an English journalist had, after years of work, solved a murder in his country. Two ministers and the director of a bank were involved in the case, which at first had been thought to be a suicide. The deceased knew too much. A horrible story. Worse than an American whodunit.

"Here," Uncle Salim remarked, "here, among us, the journalist would be dead by now."

"What exactly is a journalist?" I asked, since all I knew was that such people made newspapers somehow or other.

"Oh, a journalist," Uncle Salim replied. "A journalist is a brave and clever person. With only a piece of paper and a pencil, he strikes fear in a government, its army and police force."

"With paper and pencil," I said in astonishment, because every schoolboy has those, and we can't even impress the school janitor with them.

"Yes, he strikes fear in the government, because he is always searching for the truth, which all governments take pains to hide. A journalist is a free man, like a coachman, and, like him, lives in danger."

It would be great if I could become a journalist!

Thursday afternoon — Mahmud has a cousin who knows a lot of journalists. He works in a tavern near the newspaper and has to bring bucketfuls of coffee to them in their smoked-filled cubicles. That's not bad. I like to drink coffee and usually do so secretly, because my mother does not approve.

April 5 — Bakers' children tend to have bowlegs and tousled hair. The bowlegs come from carrying heavy loads at a young age; their tousled hair is always full of flour. The children of butchers are fat; those of locksmiths have powerful, scarred hands; the children of auto mechanics have eternally black fingernails, and so forth. I don't have to look hard at children to tell what their fathers do for a living. Only children of the rich give me trouble. They all have velvety hair and soft hands, straight legs, and don't know a thing.

A few days ago, when Josef told one of these rich brats it was no angel who had brought him into the world but his mother, who had slept with his father, the kid started to cry that his mother would never do such a thing. Josef did not let up. During recess the kid got hold of me and asked me about pregnancy, and I answered him. Then he had to listen to all the witnesses Josef produced.

Once home, the rich blockhead would not touch his food. In the evening he wanted to sleep between his mother and his father. Both of them most likely were hot for each other and were annoyed. They coaxed out of their darling son the reason for his sudden strange behavior, and the idiot told them about Josef. Today the boy's father came to school and complained about Josef, who was severely punished for allegedly having depraved the character of a child.

The father makes me sick. He sleeps with his wife, is ashamed of it, and blames it on an angel. My father cries out—far too often—that he has sired me.

April 27 — The chick that belonged to me and my little sister, Leila, grew into a splendid rooster. He was very strong and pecked at the legs of the neighbor women whenever they went to hang their wash on their terraces.

Later he even attacked my mother and my old man. The only people he left alone were me and my sister. The day before yesterday he pecked my father in the back of his head and wounded him badly. Cursing, my father got his big knife and cut the rooster's head off.

Leila turned quite pale, and I felt sick, too. My mother says the rooster's flesh is the best she ever tasted, but for two days Leila and I have been eating nothing but cheese and olives, marmalade and butter.

"I can't eat my own friend," Leila says, and she's right.

May 2 — We spent a week with my uncle in Beirut, the capital of Lebanon. It is an incredibly beautiful city on the Mediterranean coast. I love the sea. My mother is terribly afraid of the water and forbade me to go near it. But my uncle's house was so close by, and the sea is such a powerful attraction.

The first time I came back from the beach, my mother screamed at me for lying and telling her I was going to the park. My sunburned face betrayed me. So there was no dessert for me that night. The next day the sea drew me back again, but I stayed in the shade. When I came back and merrily talked about the park, my mother said, "Take off your shoes." She took them and knocked them together, and sand fell out. I lost my second dessert. That night I decided never to go back to the sea, but when I woke up the next morning, I heard the roaring surf and hurried out again. This time I was determined to fool her. I played in the water and ran around in the shade. Before I entered my uncle's house, I shook out my shoes so carefully that not a single grain of sand remained.

"What a lovely park," I announced as I walked in, smiling. My mother gave me a searching look, and I spoke even more enthusiastically about the beauty of the park's garden. She shook out my shoes, and I laughed inwardly.

Then she said, "Come here!" She took my arm and licked it. "You were in the water. Only sea salt tastes like this!"

Strangely enough, that day she gave me a double portion of vanilla ice cream.

May 15 — Just now I saw the tall, gaunt man with the sparrow, who for years has been wandering through the streets of Damascus. What a strange madman he is! And the little bird follows him like a dog. Sometimes it flutters around him, then perches on his shoulder. Whenever the bird rises into the sky, the man calls to it until the bird returns again. Sometimes the man plays tricks on the bird. He lets it sit on the walking stick he always carries and then balances the stick—with the bird perched on it—on his nose.

The madman never begs for food, but as soon as he stands at someone's door, people come out, bringing him a plate of vegetables or rice. He is very proud. He never takes anything with him. When he is satisfied, he leaves. My mother said he is probably a saint, because she has never heard of anyone besides Solomon the Wise being able to talk to birds.

Uncle Salim confirmed what my mother said about Solomon: "One day Solomon called to the birds, and they all came, except for the sparrow. Solomon called repeatedly, but the impudent sparrow came only after the third call. The wise king asked why it had not come at the first call, and the pert bird answered that it did not want to. Then Solomon the Wise cursed it: 'From this day on, you shall no longer walk like all the other birds;

instead, you shall jump!' And since then, the sparrow hops."

May 18 — Uncle Salim often tells me about a journalist who was his friend for many years. Later the man became famous, but when he was just starting out he was poor, and Uncle Salim helped him however he could. Out of gratitude the journalist wrote a long article about his friend Salim. Since Uncle Salim cannot read, he gave the newspaper to a neighbor, who read him the journalist's praise of his wisdom and generosity.

With Uncle Salim you cannot distinguish between fantastic tales and real life. Everything is so interwoven, you don't know where one thing begins and another ends. So today it was quite a surprise for me when, while telling me about something, Uncle Salim began to search for a strongbox on a shelf. He took it down and opened it. What was inside? The article! The journalist's name was Kahale. The paper has yellowed, but the article glows. I was happy to fulfill my old friend's wish; slowly and with pleasure, I read it aloud. A splendid article about a person ahead of his time. When I reached the end, Uncle Salim's eyes were filled with tears.

Saturday, June 1 — Around nine o'clock the principal came into our class. Every year he hands us our end-year evaluations himself. I already knew I would have good grades, but I had never imagined I would be first in the class. The principal praised me but emphasized that, although I could now serve as a model for the whole class, at first I had been a rather mediocre student.

My classmates listened impatiently, as they did every year; they wanted to go home, to slam their book bags into a corner and run outside. After all, it was the beginning of the holidays. But I, I couldn't get enough of his otherwise boring speech. I—the son of the baker—am first in the class! I could embrace the entire world!!! As I jubilantly burst into our courtyard, I nearly stumbled over my mother's friends, who sat with her in the shade of the tree, drinking coffee. My mother kissed me proudly and accepted with pleasure her neighbors' good wishes.

I could scarcely wait to show my father my fabulous end-year report. For now I thought I could demonstrate to him that continuing in school would be right for me.

Worming my way through the people in the bakery, I shouted the news to my father over their heads. But he paid no attention to me, no matter how much I tried to make myself conspicuous. All he cared about were the customers and his money, and then he even snapped at me, "What are you standing around for? Help this stupid Mustafa! The bread is towering up in front of him, and he drags his feet over the floor like a turtle with foot trouble. In the meantime the shelves are empty."

I knew perfectly well he did not want to listen. My father does not like school.

Enraged, I snatched a few loaves, banged them down on a shelf, and set to work. After a couple of hours in this heat, my dusty clothes stuck to my body.

Not until we were almost home, just before we came to our door, did he say: "You are first? That's good. But the bakery is a gold mine."

Again he blathered about the customers who paid him for bread, although he himself had no such sublime schooling behind him.

Why didn't I scream in his face that I hate his bakery?

Of course my mother noticed my bad mood right

away. All through dinner she talked about how the neighbors had congratulated her. As always, my father had to have the last word: "What do these stupid educators know of life? Our son will be a baker, and that's that!"

I couldn't stand it any longer. Without saying good night, I ran to my room. I do not want to be a baker! I do not want to be buried alive in a bakery! I want to travel and write! I want to be a journalist. Yes indeed, now I know it; that is my calling! I swear to God, now at 9 P.M., on Saturday, the first of June, that I will never become a baker. Never!!!

Sunday — On Sundays, after church, I am allowed to do as I like, undisturbed. But having to go to church in the first place is a bothersome duty. My father knows I don't like to go. When Sunday school is in session, we have to line up for attendance, and the religion teacher calls out each name and checks if anyone is missing. But now, despite the fact that we are on vacation, my father wants me to attend mass! Otherwise he won't give me my allowance. Josef's mother is the same. But we have a plan. One Sunday Josef will go to church, and the next Sunday I will. We'll tell each other which Gospel passage was read and what the priest preached about. For that's all our parents want to know.

I was the first to go because, idiotically enough, I drew the short straw. I always have bad luck! Today the priest gave a boring sermon about the decline of morals in Syria.

I think Jesus was very brave, throwing the merchants and money changers out of the temple like that. But there's one thing I don't understand. Why are the Jews blamed when the Romans killed him?

June 12 — My father is up to something. He said to my mother, "The boy will soon be fifteen and he still has no trade."

Over dinner a fight started. I only wanted to have a little fun, so I asked my mother if she knew how many synonyms there were in Arabic for the word *lion*. My mother didn't know a single one. I explained that there were thirty for *lion* and eighty for *dog*. She laughed heartily and said she had always known a dog was more useful than any number of lions.

My father grimaced and railed against lions, dogs, and schools that give snotty-nosed brats nothing but feeble minds. He thinks I go to school because I don't want to work in the bakery. He believes that school is made for people in the higher classes. Poor laboring devils like us have no business there. When I retorted that I've already learned a lot and that he can't even do algebra, he laughed scornfully. "Algebra!" he cried. "Who needs algebra? What I need I can calculate in my head." I am supposed to banish school from mine.

June 13 — I tried to tell my sister a horror story today. But she never gets the creeps. In the middle of the battle between the hero and a terrifying dragon, she fell asleep. I felt ridiculous.

P.S.: Leafing through these pages, I just noticed that I still haven't written a word about Nadia. I love her. She is thirteen and lives two houses down the road. Funny that I've been able to keep it a secret from my journal for so long.

June 15 — "Why school?" my father asked me. "There are too many teachers and lawyers already."

I told him I wanted to be a journalist. But he laughed

at me. He said it's a profession for good-for-nothings who sit in cafés all day, spreading lies. He doesn't want a son who runs around like a vagabond, twisting people's words and writing indecent things about them. He says we are Christians; I must get that into my head. If I were named Mohammed or Mahmud, I would only have one chance. When I asked him what he meant, he told me in a sorrowful voice that one day I would come to find out.

Nadia says she would rather marry a journalist than a baker, but she would never love anybody who worked for the secret service.

June 17 — Wow, what a wild evening at Uncle Salim's! The old man has experienced so much in his long life. One day I will write a poem about him, or a long story.

I have decided to keep my poems in a lovely notebook. I am forever losing slips of paper.

June 19 — My mother says Uncle Salim tells lies. I wish my teachers would lie a little, so their lessons would be as fascinating as Uncle Salim's stories.

June 21 — Josef has been making eyes at Nadia again, even though he knows quite well that she is my girl-friend. What a devil! I know what I'll do. Today he can tell me once again what went on in church, but next Sunday, when I'm there, he can just wonder! I'll simply tell him the wrong Gospel!

June 27 — Damn it! Mustafa, the apprentice in my father's bakery, has cleared out. I knew this was coming. In the summer nobody can stand the bakery. So I had to work there today, taking bread from the oven ledge and piling up the loaves on the shelves. My father was very nice to me. He always is when I help out in the bakery. But I can't bear this work. The steaming loaves burn your hands until you can't feel a thing. Now my palms are red and swollen. And it's so incredibly boring!

But then something funny happened. I laughed so hard I nearly wet my pants. I was supposed to assist our journeyman baker, who in the afternoon was already preparing the sourdough for the following morning. An older customer, all dressed up in a dark suit, was grumbling about the bread he had bought from us yesterday. It had become hard as bone. Naturally my father would not stand for such an affront, and so he squabbled with him for a while. Then he politely apologized and promised it would never happen again. But the customer became more and more upset and would not let my father total his receipts in peace.

In the meantime, I had climbed up on the stack of flour sacks and was trying to lower the uppermost sack so the journeyman could catch it. I grasped the stupid thing securely by its corners, but a sack like that easily weighs fifty kilos, and this one was so crammed full that it slipped right out of my hands. My fingers clutched at the seams as I tried in vain to hold on. The journeyman leaped back, and at that very moment the sack burst. The flour poured like a waterfall over the customer. A cloud of flour went up my nose, and the disgusting stuff got into my eyes. My father coughed and showered us with the choicest terms of abuse. The man stood stock-still, a living, breathing plaster cast. When my father turned and saw him, he burst out laughing.

The journeyman made the whole thing even worse. He rushed up to the speechless customer and brushed off his suit with doughy fingers. "We'll have you cleaned up right away, sir, right away," he assured him.

When I picture it to myself—the good suit full of flour, the sticky hand prints—I could laugh out loud all over again. Of course, the customer did not find any of this the least bit funny. He stormed out of the bakery, cursing.

Hopefully my father will soon find an apprentice. I cannot stand the work.

My poems look much better in the notebook.

June 29 — Today the journeyman who works at the oven said that all bakers go to heaven. When I asked him why, he answered with a laugh, "Because we already endure hell here on earth." Does he hate this work as much as I?

June 30 — Thank God! My father has finally found another apprentice. I don't have to work in the bakery any longer.

Today a fight broke out among the neighbors. Playing ball, Josef broke a neighbor's window. The wife of Nuri the florist berated Josef and his family. After only a few minutes, all the neighbor women were arguing over everything imaginable, the windowpane long forgotten. After about an hour, they were all sitting at my mother's, harmoniously drinking coffee.

July 3 — My friends and I can no longer pull the wool over my sister Leila's eyes. Once upon a time we could send her to Uncle Salim with the task of telling him to keep an eye out for his gazelle. Uncle Salim would always act surprised and say to Leila, "Well, I never, has the gazelle run away again? Come, we'll look for her together, but before we do that, I'll tell you a tale. Okay?" And Leila would become engrossed in the story and forget all about us and the gazelle. We would have the peace to enjoy our game of cards to the end.

Today, when I wanted to send her away, she said, "Uncle Salim never has had a gazelle." Just to be contrary, she sat down beside Josef, who cannot tolerate little girls anyway, and looked at his hand. Suddenly she called out, "You have three kings, but how come you only have two jacks? Eh?"

Josef almost flung his cards away. He snarled at Leila, and she bawled until he gave her a piaster. Then she went over to Mahmud. But Mahmud knows how to deal with Leila. He smooched her, and the devil only knows she can't stand that! She screeched, wiped off her cheek in disgust, and ran away.

July 5 — In the afternoons women in our neighborhood like to read coffee grounds. It's crazy! Many of them believe they can predict the future this way. I think it's funny. Nonetheless, my Aunt Warde does it best. When she does, she is so devout and earnest that it makes us laugh. She drones on and on, without moving a muscle in her face. She incorporates some of the most complicated things, and after a while she transforms the room into a fantastic landscape. Soon we are enthralled and stop interjecting stupid remarks. She speaks of the good fortune and bad that will befall us. Her voice shifts between sorrow, mourning, and joy.

Best of all, one can never tell how Aunt Warde's fortune-telling will turn out. Unlike the other women, she never feels obliged to close with a happy ending.

July 7 — Today I wrote a poem about a tree that doesn't know what it wants to be. It gets crazy leaves, at times like the moon or like swallows, because everything excites it. Its neighbors make fun of the tree.

July 10 — What is a prison compared to the bakery? My father has worked there now for more than thirty years without a break. He only took days off for his wedding and my baptism. Even when my sister Leila was baptized, he stayed in the bakery.

Every morning he's up at four, and he doesn't leave work until five in the afternoon. When he comes home, he washes, eats, then sleeps. After a few hours he gets up again, talks to us a little, and goes to the barbershop, where the men get together. When he returns home, he eats and goes back to bed. He's never awake after ten o'clock.

Day after day, summer or winter, he always rises at four o'clock without an alarm. I'd like to know how he does it. I never get out of bed until my mother has called me three times.

I once asked him about it, and he said: "When you have gotten up at four o'clock for thirty years, it's deep in your bones. You respond to an inner bell, more reliable than any Swiss clock."

Maybe he enjoys it, but it is no life for me.

July 11 — Today at two in the afternoon I saw Nadia. As usual, she smiled at me, but once again I did not trust myself to smile back. Her father was standing nearby.

I'm not the only one who's afraid of her father. The whole street seems to be more anxious since he and his family moved here. He is in the secret service. Everybody knows it. Although he wears civilian clothes, you can see his pistol under his thin summer shirt. He might just as well carry it openly; he's not fooling anyone.

P.S.: Where shall I get a job this summer? Last year I worked for a stingy goldsmith, and the summer before as a street peddler, selling sweets. My father doesn't need me in the bakery over summer vacation (thank God), but now that it is summer, I need to earn pocket money; otherwise the winter will be bad. I don't want to be in a tight spot. I would have liked to get a job with our neighborhood locksmiths, but at the moment, nobody needs an errand boy.

July 12 — After several spells of weakness—I was dizzy and did not feel well—my mother took me to a doctor. He took blood. Next Wednesday we're supposed to go back.

July 15 — Father Michael was a good man. Today he was expelled from the country because he interfered in a brawl with the police. At dawn the police set out to demolish two homes belonging to poor people. Father Michael had gotten wind of this and had spent the night with one of the families. When the cops started to use their clubs, the priest stationed himself in front of the people and stood up for them. Now and then I used to see him in his shabby old clothes, riding his bicycle. He was usually in a hurry. He always greeted us with a smile. My father knew him better, and today he was very sad that this brave man had been forced to leave our neighborhood and country.

Wednesday — I have thalassemia, a congenital Mediterranean anemia. I did not understand and asked the doctor what sort of strange illness this was. He calmed me, saying it was harmless.

My mother turned pale. She swore to the doctor that we ate meat at least twice a month. Thalassemia is hereditary, he explained, so named because *thalassa* means *sea* in Greek, and Arabs, Jews, Turks, and others who live near the Mediterranean Sea get it. However, I should eat more meat.

My mother scraped together her savings and bought two hundred grams of minced meat for me, mixed it with spices, and made several kebab skewers out of it. While the meat was frying, Leila was already grumbling that she, too, was anemic. After all, she is my sister. When my mother brought me the food, Leila looked at me with wide eyes. I couldn't get a bite down. So I divided up the skewers and swore not to touch anything before my mother also ate her share.

Uncle Salim told me where this illness comes from: "When people go hungry for decades, the sickness gets into their bones, and that's where blood is made. Then even a kebab skewer every day is no use. People need to eat their fill for centuries." He says it is stated in the Bible.

July 18 — For years Ali has been earning money off tourists. He's a rotten student—except in English, where he shines. Last summer he single-handedly earned three hundred Syrian pounds. I'll never earn that much in ten years put together. He does it in a rather clever way. My mother says I should sooner go begging in front of churches and mosques than latch onto tourists. It would ruin my character. Of course I don't believe what she says, but I'm ashamed to speak to foreigners. Ali says they are grateful to him for showing them a few places of interest and finding cheap goods and hotels for them. He gets a cut (about ten percent) from whomever he takes them to, but sometimes he has to beat it when the tourist authorities appear; they don't look kindly upon his activities. He also has quite a few addresses, and now and then he gets a postcard from someone.

July 20 — Five days ago Uncle Salim helped me find employment with Ismat the cabinetmaker, a remarkable fellow. I like wood, so I'm very pleased. Ismat's workshop was like a rubbish dump the first day; it took me two days to straighten it up. Since then I've had less to do, and Ismat grumbles continually that he can't find anything now. But he never grumbles if I do nothing at all for hours. He works very slowly and sings the whole time in a rather peculiar way. When he arrives in the morning, he starts singing a song and repeats it all day long. For ten hours he hums or sings this one tune, even the same words. At the end of an entire day spent working on a small table for a farmer, he seems to feel very satisfied with himself and his labors. He likes the tea I make for him and lets me have some, but he gets angry when I hammer a nail too much.

Only one client gets on my nerves. She comes by every day and asks about the bedroom furniture for her daughter, who is engaged to be married. Ismat consoles her anew each time. So far, I have still not seen any sign of a bedroom set. But today Ismat promised her that the magnificent bedroom would be ready next week.

July 21 — Josef is sick and tired of the construction site where he worked last summer. He wants to copy Ali and go hunting for tourists. Ali let him tag along for two days and learn the essentials. Now all Josef talks about is how easy it is to earn money. Unlike Ali, he does not respect the tourists. He thinks they're dense.

Today Mahmud and I teased Josef. When we ran into him in the company of an old, much made-up American woman, we addressed him in English.

He blushed deep red. Josef speaks such wretched English, I asked him how he manages.

"Well, do you really believe the tourists want to know anything intelligent? All they ever ask is what something is and how much it costs. You can get that English down in two days."

July 25 — Today I finished constructing a treasure chest, consisting of three boxes, for my sister. I've been working on it in secret for days; Ismat hasn't noticed a thing. At lunchtime I brought it to her. She was thrilled.

The bedroom woman came back and screamed at Ismat. He paid her no mind and simply went on singing. The song could be transcribed this way: "When you're going up a mountain, you need not have a care; the peak is coming soon, and then it's easy to slide down."

The woman snapped that if he wasn't through by next week, *she* would sing a song for *him*.

July 30 — Thank God we haven't seen the woman for five days. Ismat's lying to her embarrasses me. For five days we have been working away from the shop, at the house of a rich merchant. He gave Ismat the task of restoring a valuable wooden door in his gorgeous house Today we finished it. A masterpiece. Ismat has really done a marvelous job. You can't even tell that a few days ago the door was practically falling apart. He carved a few pieces by hand. The man's wife and only son kept jeering that Ismat was repairing a whole pyramid and not just a simple door. Ismat took his time and continually demanded tea. But the man was so satisfied that he gave Ismat much more than they had agreed upon, and he also stuck five more pounds into my pocket. (For a whole week of work at Ismat's all I earn is four!)

August 1 — Today it happened! I knew it would not go well.

An incredible story: The woman came about ten in the morning. She demanded Ismat either deliver the bedroom furniture or return her three-hundred-pound deposit. Ismat made fun of her and sang his song about going up and down the mountain. Then the lady went wild. She took the warmed-up pot of glue, overturned it on Ismat's head, and threatened to come back every day and pour a pot of glue over him until the bedroom set was finished; she stormed out in a rage.

Ismat calmly sat down on a chair and said I should get the police. He acted as if he didn't notice the glue, which slowly ran down his head, over his shoulders, into his lap, and fell in drops to the floor. I was confused by his behavior and ran as fast as I could to the nearest police station. But the officer on duty was very busy and made me wait for more than three hours. When he finally heard the story, he wanted to throw me out, but I swore I wasn't making it up. When we arrived in the workshop, the glue had dried, and Ismat was still sitting in the chair. The officer stared at him speechless, as if he were gazing upon a little man from Mars. Then with his finger he tapped on the stuff that covered Ismat's head like a crash helmet, and murmured, "Hard, hard!"

"Mr. Officer, the woman attacked me in my own work-shop!" Ismat wailed.

"And why, if you will permit me the question?" the officer shrieked.

"Because the wood for her bedroom set has still not arrived."

"In this country, the best that can happen is that you go crazy; only then are you happy!" the officer groaned. He pounded his fist on the table. "The government lets the wood rot in the harbor. The daughter won't marry without a particular bedroom set. I spend an entire day with a drunken tourist who has thrown up in the middle of the mosque. And I can't even hit him since he comes from an allied country. The woman tips a pot of glue over his noggin, and the dopey carpenter lets it dry. Have you got witnesses?"

This was all too much for me. I thought, Now both of them have gone nuts.

"Yes, the boy can testify," Ismat answered calmly.

"But he is under eighteen, and his testimony won't be valid," the officer objected and began to write in his note-book. Ismat stood up and tried to wash the glue off with water. It didn't work.

"Try a chisel," the officer recommended venomously. He inquired about the woman's address and left.

August 2 — Today Ismat came to work with a scarf over his head. He didn't say a word. When his headdress slipped a little, I saw his head was shaved clean!

August 3 — Now I have given five pounds to my mother and one to my sister. But neither of them will let me in on why they wanted the money.

August 4 — I have more than fifteen pounds! My mother is beside herself because yesterday I bought her a pair of stockings. She wept for joy. She had never been able to afford such good ones. Today I brought her a pound of coffee. After supper my father drank a cup, and my mother proudly told him I had given it to her. He looked at me in astonishment.

"My clever little carpenter," he said to me before going to bed.

August 5 — For once I'd like to know what my mother is up to. She seems to be planning some sort of surprise for me. Each time I come in the door, she dashes out of the room, as if she had something to hide.

August 9 — Nadia was nowhere to be seen today. I haven't caught sight of her for two days! When I came home, again my mother scurried out of the room. But I noticed bits of blue cloth lying around. Good heavens, I think I know what her surprise is!

August 11 — I was right! My mother may well be the best mother in the world, but, unfortunately, she is also the worst seamstress. Are these supposed to be pajamas? The sleeves are far too short, and the top is so tight at my waist, I look like a scarecrow inside it! The pants are so big and broad, there's enough room for me and an elephant! I told my mother she must have a soft spot in her heart for animals. We laughed until we cried.

August 15 — The woman never returned. She let the police know she would forfeit the deposit if Ismat would withdraw his complaint. Today Ismat was summoned to the police station. When he came back, he laughed triumphantly and sang. His hair is beginning to grow back a little.

August 16 — August in Damascus is unbearably hot. During the day the temperature sometimes reaches 42 degrees Celsius in the shade. At night it's so hot we can't sleep. Often I wake up because the bed pricks me as if it were studded with nails. Then, like many others, I sit on the terrace to try and catch the faintest breeze. Damascus is very peaceful at night. At dawn *muezzins* from hundreds of minarets used to call people to prayer with their "*Allāhu Akbar,* God is most Great." Nowadays they leave cassette players running in front of loudspeakers, and the brief delays between starting up the many tape players cause the call to echo a hundred times. Sometimes I fall asleep on the terrace and get a stiff neck.

August 17 — Uncle Salim does not let tourists photograph him. Somehow these idiots love him in his Arab attire. With his big moustache, he looks terrifying.

Today I asked him why he covers his face with his hands when the tourists pull out their cameras. He said he once permitted it and afterwards was ill for a very long time. The camera had snatched something out of his soul.

Well, sometimes he exaggerates a little.

August 18 — Today the police were at Ali's parents' place. They rummaged through the apartment. Then one of them waited until Ali returned and took him along to the station. A tourist alleged that Ali had stolen his expensive camera. The police had pretty well beat Ali black and blue by the time the tourist found his stupid camera in a bar. Ali was free to go home. The police made him sign a paper that said he would not speak to tourists anymore. But by the following afternoon, Ali was back out hunting.

August 20 — How Josef manufactures his toys so cleverly out of a heap of wire is a mystery to me. From remnants he's begged off people, he constructs steerable cars and airplanes, houses with windows and doors that open and close, genuine small works of art. When I was able to get two ball bearings from the auto mechanic, Josef helped me build a skateboard. But today I had bad luck. I was on the skateboard, and it made a hellish noise. Still, I was content and sang at the top of my lungs until a wasp stung the tip of my tongue. My tongue swelled up so much I could barely speak. My mother laughed at me and said she wanted to buy two candles for the saints of the wasps, who had finally granted peace to her ears by silencing my mouthpiece.

August 22 — We all met at Mahmud's place because his parents had gone to somebody's wedding. He got the idea to seal our friendship from a film. I like it a lot. Mahmud, Josef, and I—the inseparable three—will found a gang that fights for justice. We already have a name for ourselves: the Black Hand. That was Josef's suggestion. We have sworn never to betray one another. Josef pronounced the oath, and Mahmud and I repeated it in a half-darkened room.

"Whom are we against?" Josef asked, pulling out his ball-point pen, which he keeps with him at all times, even when he's in pajamas. I did not want to be against anyone unconditionally. But Josef said a gang always must be against someone; otherwise, it is not a gang. We agreed to be against the secret service man and the grocer who always cheats our mothers.

August 24 — Yesterday we met at Josef's and drew up our first letter. It was for the secret service man. *The Black Hand is warning you! If you file one more report against a resident of this street, you will have to deal with us, Spy!* We thought this message would scare enough respect into him that he'd finally leave us in peace.

But I was the one who was supposed to tack it up on his door. I didn't want to, since, after all, he is Nadia's father and I like her so much. But the others said, "First justice, then love." Mahmud would actually have given in because he knows how important Nadia is to me, but Josef insisted. He said each of us had to demonstrate his courage.

"I'm no coward; I'll do it," I screamed and ran home from Josef's. But I couldn't sleep all night, and I didn't go to Ismat's today either. All day long I was sullen. How could I ever explain this to Nadia if she found out? Tonight is my final deadline; otherwise, my cowardice will bar me from the Black Hand. The folded piece of paper is in the pocket of my trousers; it is so hot, it seems made of fire. Perhaps Nadia will forgive me.

August 26 — Last night I stuck the paper on the door. Josef walked by afterward to make sure the task had been carried out. But he hung around Nadia's house a long time. I wonder what more he wanted there.

This morning the paper was gone. Had the secret service man read it? I tried not to get too close to Nadia. I was thoroughly ashamed of myself.

Josef and Mahmud praised me for my bravery.

August 27 — Today Nadia said her father read a letter that threw him into a rage. He thinks it came from an underground organization. Nadia doesn't know who wrote it, but she seems to savor her father's exasperation. We gang members celebrated the news. Mahmud wanted to tack up a second note himself, on which there would be just one word—*Wait!* But Josef and I refused. First we want to see what happens.

August 31 — In the last few days everything on our street has been topsy-turvy. I couldn't even sit down to write. The secret service man is really on edge. He told the greengrocer that experts are now analyzing the ink and the handwriting. I got scared, but Josef calmed me down. He said he knew the spy had no leads. And from my lovely handwriting, one automatically thinks of an adult and not a boy of fourteen years.

I dreamed armed police troops surrounded the block and that I was led through the streets with my hands bound and my shirt wide open. The neighbors waved to me with their handkerchiefs, and when I passed Nadia, she ran up to me and threw herself, sobbing, around my neck. The truck that would take me to prison was waiting at the end of the street; the guards trembled in fear. Suddenly Uncle Salim came riding on a white horse, and behind him came a powerful-looking man on a black one. Clearly, he was one of the thieves from Uncle Salim's stories.

Today I don't know whether this was a real dream or a story I made up.

September 1 — Today I made a beautiful Chinese lantern out of an orange. I removed the flesh through a hole at the top, then carved little windows in the rind and put a candle inside. Shining through the pores, the light looks as if it came from thousands of small, yellowish lamps.

September 3 — We have been deliberating over which of the other boys should be in our gang and have come to the conclusion that Ali is the only possibility.

September 4 — I asked Ali whether he wanted to join the Black Hand. He laughed at me, saying he was a tourist-catcher, not a bandit, but he could give us an assignment. His friend Georg had borrowed three pounds from him and now denied it. If we beat Georg up and got the money back, one of those three pounds would be ours.

Josef is enthusiastic at the prospect of improving our finances and wants to accept the commission, but Mahmud and I are against it. What's between Georg and Ali is no concern of ours. We are a justice gang, not personal cops.

September 5 — Nadia was waiting for me on the corner. I like her more and more.

September 7 — "Why are you always running away?" Nadia asked me today. She had also been waiting on the corner a few days ago, but I had run past her. She had laughed so sweetly! If only she had a different father!

September 9 — Nadia wants us to meet secretly. I told her I don't want to. How can I say I'm afraid of her father?

September 11 — For days my old man has been bitching about the bad flour.

Uncle Salim said something beautiful today. While he

was telling a story from his youth, Josef's mother, sitting in our courtyard peeling potatoes, accused him of exaggerating. "You mean to say that I'm lying?" Uncle Salim asked calmly. "But falsehood is the twin sister of truth. No sooner does one appear than you can see the other; all you need are good eyes."

The woman tittered; they didn't understand him as I did. A fabulous remark.

September 13 — This Mahmud, nothing escapes him. Today I quickly stroked Nadia's hair, and she blushed. That scoundrel Mahmud came to me and said some time ago he had noticed what was going on between us. If I went on publicly courting the secret service man's daughter, he'd be happy to attend my engagement party—in jail.

September 15 — Mahmud is always asking questions! Today we saw an American movie—a great mystery. Afterward Mahmud was upset. When I asked him the reason, he said, "Hasn't it occurred to you that all the criminals are shady characters with black hair and ugly mugs? Why is this so? Why isn't a handsome blond man ever a criminal? Then the films would be more exciting! After five minutes I know who committed the murder, but the detective is so dumb, he needs two hours to figure it out."

September 17 — God, was it ever painful for the neighbors today! The miller stood outside our door and yelled for my father. My mother had to say he wasn't at home. The miller didn't believe her, so he spoke with her as if my father were within earshot. He threatened to stop delivering flour if he didn't get his money by next Tuesday.

Nadia thinks my poem about the flying tree is very pretty. Because of my handwriting, I could not give her a copy. All I need is for her father to see it!

September 18 — I'll probably never see the inside of school again. At supper my father said he can't manage alone anymore and why, after all, had he brought a boy into this world who would not help him. But I don't want to go into the bakery business, cost what it may. When my father's voice got really loud, Uncle Salim came up to our apartment. He said he had come to visit me, his friend. My mother was glad to see him because my father has great respect for him. Amazing that Uncle Salim is never ashamed of my friendship, even when my father, in his wrath, counts me the worst of scoundrels.

How often I wish Uncle Salim never should die.

September 20 — Today I had a good idea. I wanted the Black Hand to write a threatening letter to my father so he would not take me out of school. Mahmud wrote a few lines:

Dear Sir, Not that we have anything against you, but you simply must not take your clever son out of school. It would be expressly against the will of our gang. In spite of the love we have for you, we must warn you against it!

I thought the message sounded stupid. We might as well have been inviting my old man to a party! I suggested we use stronger language and really make a threat, but Mahmud refused. He respects my father more than his own.

Josef sneered at the word *clever*. I told him straight out that he's just plain jealous that I'm first in the class. We argued quite a bit.

"This gang shits," he cried, "if all it aims to do is solve its members' family problems." He walked out.

I've had enough. A gang that doesn't even want to protect its own members! Mahmud suggested we secede and let Josef go on by himself.

Funny, we are the best of friends, but our gang has not yet survived one autumn. How do adults do it?

September 21 — "The mosques are built of marble, while our shacks crumble and hurl their clay on our heads. The sun plays in the courtyards of the mosques, and people suffocate in damp, dark holes." Enraged, Mahmud told me about his uncle who lives with his entire family in one room. The room has only one window, which once looked onto open space, affording the family some light and air. Now a rich sheik from Saudi Arabia has erected a mosque in the space. The high walls of the new building are so close to the houses that they block the view from all the windows. The protests of the community do no good, for the sheik has powerful friends.

For a year Mahmud's uncle has not gone into the mosque.

September 22 — The street merchants always extol their wares in a splendid way, which is sometimes also comical. The masters among them are the sellers of fruits and vegetables.

"A hiccup after every bite! Quinces!"

"In you nests the dew, Figs!"

"My tomatoes painted their cheeks and went for a stroll!"

"The bees will go pale with envy! Honey melons!"

Only the tarragon, which we get cheaply and fresh and

have on our table at lunch every day, comes off badly.

"Tarragon, you traitor!"

Why traitor? I asked my mother, and she said that tarragon grows not only where you plant it but also creeps under the earth and turns up in your neighbors' field.

All the merchants exaggerate. Not only do they seem to care for their fruits conscientiously; they even seem to know them personally. Some of them grossly overstate all the things they have stuck in the ground on behalf of their mangy heads of lettuce.

The man who sells fish is the true master of embellishment. Over and over again he talks about a huge fish he once caught in a distant sea. It irritates Uncle Salim.

"The fish weighed 120 kilos and 150 grams!" the fish seller reported. It's not the 120 kilos but the ridiculous 150 grams that bother my old friend!

"This I don't believe!" Uncle Salim says. "It was at most 120 kilos and 10 grams on the scale!"

The two strange old birds argued over it a long time.

September 25 — Today we gave it to an old tourist. He came strolling down our street with his wife and wanted to photograph us—all ten of us kids. We grinned into the camera. He took several shots, while fat Georg ran around wildly with Hassan. The stupid fool pulled out a dollar bill and told Georg that the money would be his if he knocked Hassan to the ground. Georg doesn't understand a word of English, but upon seeing the green bill immediately figured out what the guy wanted. For a piaster, Georg would even throw his mother to the ground! He was on the verge of running after slightly built Hassan again, but Josef was quicker. He grabbed Georg around the neck and cried out to the tourist in

English, "No! I'll give two dollars to watch your wife box your ears. Then I'll take the picture!"

Josef lunged for the man's camera. The man's wife laughed heartily. In Arabic I explained to Georg why the man looked so appalled. The idiot was so pleased that he rammed into the man's side and ran off. The man staggered around and had a hard time keeping our dirty hands away from his camera and out of his trouser pockets. Cursing, he ran down the street.

September 26 — Today Georg made me lose my salary (all four pounds). That swine! Gone, my money and my dream of going to the movies.

I was standing outside his door, raving about the film I wanted to see.

"Do you want to double your money?" he suddenly asked me.

"What kind of question is that!" I replied. "Of course!" Idiot that I am.

"You know Toni, the gynecologist's son. He likes to bet and has a lot of money. He's got bundles of bills in his pocket, so what difference does the loss of a pound make to him? Eh? None whatsoever. A stupid boy. He says he can guess all the cards without touching them. Before your very eyes he buys a new deck of cards. You shuffle them; then he looks at the pile and tells you what the top ten cards are. He claims things always go his way."

"And what happens when they don't?"

"If he gets one wrong, you win. I don't know whether he's telling tales or whether what the others say is true," the lousy creep whispered, knowing exactly how to suck me in.

"What do the others say?"

"That his father gives him X-ray pills so his eyes can even see through walls."

"Rubbish! But tell me, why don't you double your own money?"

"All I have is a few piasters, and Toni won't take a bet under one pound," he said.

"Good, let's go!" I had become curious about this dunce.

"But what's in it for me? After all, I'm the one who told you about it. Three piasters for every pound you win?"

"One piaster. No more. It's my money that's at risk."

Georg accepted, and we walked to Olive Lane. There the fat hippo Toni stood at the edge of a little playground. But he didn't want to play. He said he'd just lost three times and now he didn't feel like it.

Georg implored him, and Toni finally agreed under one condition, that I pay for the next deck of cards. To myself I thought, what difference does buying the cards make if I win? So I went to the shop around the corner and bought a deck of cards for one pound.

I really must be uniquely stupid. I could kick myself. No ram in the world is so dumb as to also bring the butcher a knife.

I opened the pack and shuffled the cards for a long time; then I laid the neat, tidy stack on one of the stairs. I gave Georg one pound to hold, and Toni drew a thick wad of bills out of his pocket and also handed Georg a bill.

"Withdrawing from the bet counts as a loss," Toni said, as though he were an old hand. Then he gazed at the pile and whispered, "Queen."

I turned the card over, and in fact it was a queen.

Again the hippo concentrated, and I thought, now Lady Luck will deal him a blow for his arrogance. But my fingers went stiff when I turned over a jack, just as Toni had predicted. Ten times he guessed right, and I lost the pound.

A donkey avoids the pit it has once fallen into, but I? I stumbled even more willfully into the next catastrophe. I raised the stakes to two pounds. Toni invited me to buy new cards, but since he hadn't laid a finger on the old ones, I didn't want to. I made Georg stand farther away from me. Some people bring bad luck. I wanted to know if that's what the problem was. I shuffled the cards thoroughly; then I laid them on the step. Again Toni guessed correctly ten times.

I sat there as if paralyzed. Georg excused himself and disappeared, and Toni trotted away, content. I was shaking with rage, at Georg and above all at myself.

I walked home slowly. En route I saw Georg licking a big ice cream cone. He smiled peculiarly and quickly looked away.

When I told Mahmud about the X-ray pills, he laughed and told me what an idiot I was. He explained that the place where I bought the deck sells only marked cards. On the back of each one, in the chaos of the colorful pattern, is a small sign that tells what each card is. Mahmud owns a deck of these cards. After a short time I also knew how to distinguish the thirteen different signs from one another.

Mahmud wanted to beat up Georg right away, but after a while we came up with a better plan. A completely diabolical plan! Georg won't notice a thing. All we need is five pounds. Mahmud and I are broke just now, so we'll see if Uncle Salim will advance us the sum.

September 27 — We've paid them back for what they did to me. We robbed Toni outright. He'll never speak to Georg again.

Uncle Salim was splendid and gave us the five Syrian pounds with no questions asked. Mahmud flashed the bills under Georg's eyes until Georg lured him to Toni. Mahmud followed him to the playground like a pious lamb.

Once there, he went to the shop, but all he bought was a pack of chewing gum. He took a fresh deck of un-marked cards out of his trouser pocket and returned to the playground.

Mahmud opened the pack of cards and cried out loudly, so all the children within earshot could hear, "You know, I'm absolutely positive you'll lose, so I'm betting five pounds. If you're not a coward, you'll put up five as well."

Smiling, Toni accepted the bet. Mahmud shuffled the cards, beaming at Georg, who looked a bit unsettled. "Come on, be my good luck charm," he said, kissing Georg on the cheek. The boys in the playground drew nearer and ogled the ten pounds Georg held in his hand. Mahmud put the cards on the step.

Toni looked for a long time.

"Well, X-ray Eye, will you be done soon?" Mahmud taunted him.

Finally Toni said, "Two of hearts."

Mahmud turned it over.

It was the ten of diamonds.

"Let's have that money, Good Luck Charm!" Mahmud bellowed and snatched the cards away before the con-fused Toni could pick them up. "I'll give you one more chance, but you may not touch the cards."

"One moment, please," the hippopotamus pleaded.

"So, now you're scared, eh? No, if you're not a sissy, come up with ten pounds!"

"Ten pounds!" the others gasped.

Toni preferred to go into the shade, claiming the sun had blinded him.

"If you like, but now that you've accepted the bet, I just want to stress you can no longer back out!"

Toni put up the ten pounds and was defeated by the first card. Mahmud kissed Georg and gave him a piaster. "That's what we arranged, isn't it?" he called loudly.

Georg seemed about to remind Mahmud that his cut was one piaster per pound and not per fifteen, but he swallowed hard when he saw the look on Toni's face.

We bought Uncle Salim two packets of the very finest tobacco for his water pipe. It cost three pounds a pack. The remaining nine pounds we divided among us.

September 28 — When I told Uncle Salim the whole story today, I remarked that I felt like examining every would-be friend with a magnifying glass before I called him a real friend. Uncle Salim shook his head.

"And if inspection reveals you've made three hundred mistakes? Seek out new friends, and don't be suspicious!" He sucked on his water pipe. "You know, my friend, it's the poor in this world who invented friendship. The powerful have no need of it. They have their power. Seek out friends, and let the magnifying glass alone. Using it could be the biggest mistake of your life: You will live alone."

September 29 — I ran through the fields with Nadia today. I gave her a kiss, and we laughed about our parents.

I gave two pounds to Leila. And she's already spent it.

Today was also my last day at the cabinetmaker's. Working with him was a lot of fun, and now I know how to handle wood. Not a single window in our apartment sticks anymore.

Tomorrow evening I want to go with Mahmud to see the film at the new cinema in town.

October 10 — A few days ago we accompanied a very congenial young man from Luxembourg to the airport. His name was Robert, and he was twenty-one years old. Not only did he steal our hearts but those of our mothers as well.

Hunting for tourists, Josef picked him up in front of the church and attempted to ensnare him with his usual spiel, saying, "My mother is sick, and I have to feed the entire family. My uncle makes lovely wooden boxes and copper plates," and everything else he had by heart. But Robert spoke to him in Arabic, saying he did not want to buy either boxes or plates. He had no money, and he was extremely hungry.

Josef invited him to eat, and they liked each other at once. We got to meet him, too, and fetched his things from the hotel. Everyone took him in for a few days, my family included. My father said the door should always be open to foreigners and that Robert could share my room with me. My sister was permitted to crawl into our parents' bed during this time. Leila didn't like Robert and was always asking him when he would leave. Robert, good soul that he was, laughed at her and replied, "Never!"

He was received in the same way at Mahmud's and at Josef's. Only Ali said he would have no part of it; tourists really ought not to see our poor homes. We were grateful that it was Josef and not Ali who had met this wonderful guy. I think Robert loved us—and even my mother liked him to distraction. Every morning she told me to take good care of him. She made such a fuss over him, you would think he was made of chocolate.

Robert had grown up in Egypt, where his father had worked for fifteen years. Then he returned to Luxembourg (I was ashamed I had never heard of Luxembourg, but Robert said it's only a tiny little state anyhow). When he'd finished his studies there, he decided to spend one month of each year in an Arab country. Next year he wants to travel to North Yemen.

What I especially like about Robert is that he's a sly fox. One day he lost his wallet, but he refused to report it to the police (he cannot tolerate the police). He laughed and said, "If you lose money but find such friends as you, then you've won." Two days later, the wily Luxembourger came up with a good idea. He would put on clean clothes and comb his hair and lie in wait for tourists. He wanted to pass himself off as the son of a Luxembourgian ambassador in Cairo, who only occasionally spent a few days in Damascus. He had it all worked out: Tourists would very quickly trust him because he was blond and spoke four languages perfectly. He would then accompany them to shops run by our friends; later we would get ten percent of the price of everything the tourists bought. He put his plan in action, and it went very smoothly. We spent the money like lunatics. We ate at the best restaurant. And he also brought home trophies from his hunting expeditions, in the form of small presents.

But the best things were our conversations with him. He told us about children in Europe, and we were astonished to learn that things often go no better for them than for us. Certainly, they have a lot more chocolate, but many fewer playgrounds and less free time. Their parents hit them, too (though somewhat less openly, resulting in fewer kisses). No, we should not envy them. Or maybe we should, in one regard, namely that child labor is prohibited. I find that good. In Europe parents must be able to feed their families without the help of their children.

Two days before his departure, Robert had his hair cut. He gave each of us a blond lock and said when we think of him, we should stroke it. Wherever he might be, he would feel our hands. A crazy fellow, but while writing these last lines, I took the little box out of the drawer and stroked the soft hair.

October 11 — School has started again. We have the same teachers as before. My old man seems to have forgotten that he's forbidden me to go to school. Since our last argument, I try to keep out of his way.

I like our Arabic teacher and our history teacher better than all the others. Mr. Katib has been instructing us in Arabic for a year now. He is rather old and extremely funny. Very often he sits in a corner, reading a book, even while we're taking an exam. He never goes into the staff room during recess; instead, he sits by himself under the big weeping willow in the schoolyard and reads. Once I crept close and watched him. He becomes wholly engrossed in his book; sometimes he cries, then he laughs out loud and slaps his thigh, so that anyone who sees him simply laughs along too. Mahmud says Mr. Katib has a good heart, and this is no exaggeration. He always gives us the best grades. Once he told us he had experienced difficulties in other schools for this reason.

He enjoys teaching in our school because the principal is a decent man.

Our history teacher is a Palestinian. Mr. Maruf may be young, but he's really good. He's a tireless, interesting lecturer who gives tough exams. He is also the only teacher who bitches about all the Arab governments. If I weren't going to be a journalist, becoming a teacher wouldn't be bad at all.

October 12 — There was another coup today. School will be closed till next Monday. This is the second time schools have closed this year.

In Damascus coups like these generally start at dawn. We who live in the old quarter first get wind of what's happening on the radio. Suddenly everything's quiet; then brisk military music comes on, and then the new government's communiqués—full of charges against the old government—are broadcast.

Uncle Salim just now told me that fifteen years ago, during the first coup, he believed what the new government promised. He rejoiced and celebrated until dawn. At the time of the second coup, he merely applauded. Since the third, all he can do is shake his head.

My father came home and talked about his fears. "The new government talks about war too much."

I hate war and am afraid of it, too.

Nadia's father is still a secret service man—perhaps higher up. What a traitor! As of today, he is in the employ of the opponents of yesterday's government. How he can do this is completely beyond me.

October 18 — School is open. Our history teacher, Mr. Maruf, has vanished. Nobody knows whether he was imprisoned or if he fled. Soon we'll get someone else. If only the bio-boxer would leave! I can't stand this thug of a biology teacher; he forbids us to ask any questions and hits us, even though it's prohibited. Sometimes I dream of getting up and telling him I think he's dumb. Then he can thrash me, for all I care. But it's only a dream. I haven't yet dared say it.

At least our congenial Arabic teacher is still with us.

October 25 — Autumn is the season I like best. Damascus is at its most beautiful. Swallows fill the sky with their vivid cries, as if anxious to reap the last joys before setting out on their long journey south. The streets are full of peddlers, extolling their fall fruits. There aren't as many tourists as in summer, and the few who are here seem to take a genuine interest in our everyday life.

Today an old lady looked through the door to our house, which is always open, and saw my mother preparing stuffed eggplants. She politely asked me what they were. I explained in dreadful English, and she asked if she might come a bit closer. My mother, embarrassed about her old dress, was afraid the woman wanted to photograph her. But the lady had no camera. I calmed my mother down, and the woman admired her skillful hands.

And I don't have to help my father in the bakery so often in the fall. After harvesttime many farmers and agricultural workers, now unemployed, stream into the city in search of work. My father gets more applicants than he needs. I can properly concentrate on school, and once school is out, my time is my own. And Nadia's!!!

October 28 — We've had chemistry for one year now. Today the old oddball teacher wanted to take us into the laboratory. News of this nearly triggered a disturbance.

Everybody wanted to make a stink bomb, but nobody wanted to sit in the first row.

Before recess, the teacher called Mahmud, Josef, and me up to his desk. Since we all live near the school, he wanted one of us to rush home and get a hard-boiled egg for an experiment demonstrating a vacuum. Mahmud said his mother had no eggs, but if a potato would do, he could bring a splendid one. Josef, the old fox, said his family never ate eggs because all of them were allergic. I was trapped. My last grade in chemistry wasn't exactly the best, and I wanted to make a good impression. I hurried home.

But when I asked my mother, she gaped at me, horrified. "What a strange teacher you have. Instead of books, he uses eggs for his lessons!"

I had a hard time explaining to her what a vacuum is. "Vacuum?" she repeated. "Eggs are for cooking; the teacher should make his vacuum with something else." After a while she reluctantly gave me a small egg. She suspected I wanted to sell it and buy some cigarettes with the money.

The egg was as small as a pigeon's. I boiled it, and by the time I reached the schoolyard, recess was over. We went into the lab, whose plentiful glassware and equipment give it a mysterious air. We squeezed ourselves into the last three rows, and the teacher paraded up and down like a peacock, as if enjoying our cowardice.

He told us something about a vacuum, peeled the egg, and tossed some cotton into a bottle with a long, wide neck; then he poured in some alcohol and ignited it. He explained that when he stoppered the bottle with the egg, and the fire had consumed all the oxygen, a vacuum would be created, causing the egg to be sucked into the bottle. "Without a vacuum, the egg would not go into the bottle," he said, holding the egg over the neck. Unaware of what he was doing, he let the egg fall, and it smoothly slid through. The class howled.

"You don't need a vacuum for that, just small eggs!" Isam called out.

The teacher was furious; he wanted to extract the egg and try a different flask, but the egg got wedged crosswise in the neck. He cursed and shook the bottle hard. The alcohol sprayed out, and suddenly the egg flew smack into the wall and fell down, smashed. The laboratory smelled like a tavern.

November 2 — Mahmud is incredibly brave. Today he dared ask the bio-boxer a question. (This fool doesn't like us to ask him anything.) It concerned the difference between human sperm and eggs, and the biology teacher did not answer it. Instead, he took pains to show Mahmud what a bad student he was, and his speech ended in a reprimand.

"Do you have another question?" he sneered cynically.

Mahmud looked at him and answered, "Now I have two. The first, the one you did not answer, has given birth to a second."

The bio-boxer flipped. He slapped Mahmud. "And now?"

"Now there are four," Mahmud exclaimed.

We all cried out "bravo" so loud that the teacher refrained from carrying out what was certainly his plan, to thrash Mahmud even more.

During recess Isam swore that if the thug had touched Mahmud one more time, he would have strangled him. That would have been something! The Class Colossus against the Bio-Boxer. We would have understood Darwin as never before.

November 4 — Mr. Katib let us freely choose a theme and develop it as a poem, story, or fable. I will offer him two poems from my collection.

November 7 — Our religion teacher really got hot under the collar today. Josef asked him—as vulgarly as only he can: What is the significance of the seal of confession? The teacher stressed that as a priest, he is forbidden to betray or exploit this seal of confidentiality when someone makes confession.

Josef went on to ask what he would do if someone confessed he had placed a bomb in the confessional. The priest said of course he would remain seated and not exploit the seal of confession. Then the entire class burst out laughing, because everyone knows the priest is a scaredy-cat. Finally he admitted he would flee after all, because doing so would harm no one.

Josef immediately cried out, "You can't do that; you'd be exploiting the seal of confession!"

The priest's sole reply was: "For next time you will copy out the story of the creation three times."

I must tell this to Nadia. Surely she too will laugh about Josef's bad luck.

November 9 — Of all heavenly bodies I love the moon most. Not just the full moon, but even the smallest sliver of the moon instills in me a special kind of peace. Uncle Salim said that when his grandfather looked at the moon, he was able to predict whether or not it would rain. If only the all-seeing moon would tell me whether I'll manage to do well on my biology exam. Certainly the moon thinks the bio-boxer is just as stupid as I do.

November 13 — Today Mahmud told me the story of how the madman silenced a scholar. Mahmud and his father went to the nearby mosque to say Friday prayers. The madman stood at the big fountain, washing his hands, feet, and face, just like the other believers. His sparrow also cleaned itself happily and then perched atop a pole. The madman seated himself rather far back in the mosque, and Mahmud nearly forgot about him until the service began.

The scholar leading the congregation was an indignant critic in general. He disparaged all religions other than Islam and aggressively attacked all Islamic sects that did not subscribe to Sunnite precepts. Suddenly the madman stood up and intoned a long "amen" in an incredibly beautiful voice. Then he proceeded to sing a rhythmical religious song, extolling the divinity of mankind and love for all living things. The song made such an impression that the faithful sang the stanzas with him.

The scholar was struck dumb. To be sure, several times he tried to regain the floor, but his voice was drowned out by the loud singing. Foaming with rage, he had the madman dragged out by two servants. You could hear him go on singing, even though his mouth was being held shut. The members of the congregation settled down again and were quickly led to the end of the prayer.

What a pity they didn't follow the madman!

November 14 — Today was one of the loveliest days of my life. Our double period in Arabic was so powerful, I've never experienced anything like it. We all presented our themes extemporaneously. Mr. Katib sat among us, and enthusiastically discussed or disputed our stories, fables, and poems. When it was my turn, I recited "I Dreamed Aloud" and "The Flying Tree"; I know my poems by heart. The teacher found them extraordinarily good and remarked that a poet was speaking from inside me. I felt myself blush a deep red. Mahmud said I spoke well, even if sometimes I declaimed so loudly he nearly got an earache.

When the class period was up, we even continued into the break, so that the remaining five students could recite. Previously, something like this was unimaginable in my class; we always have one foot in the schoolyard before the bell rings.

Now I'm tired, but tomorrow I absolutely have to record Mahmud's presentation. It was unique!

November 15 — Mahmud wrote a play entitled *The Letters of the Alphabet.* It portrays a young teacher who decides to teach the people who live on his street how to read. He is very stupid and treats the old men and women like snot-nosed little brats. When they come for the first lesson, the people are curious. Tired from a long day of work, they go to a room in a nearby school and wait for the teacher. After having sounded the bell, he arrives in a suit and tie, carrying a walking stick. He asks the people to stand up. Many of them do, but a proud old farmer says he has only risen in someone's presence twice in his life, once when the bishop visited him, and the second time when Sultan Abdülhamid rode past his field.

The teacher mulishly begins to discuss the letters of the alphabet. He draws an *A* and tells them to impress this form on their minds. When he gets to the letter *C*, a woman wants to know if *laundry day* has a *C* in it. A butcher asks how to spell *cattle*. The farmer asks a question like the butcher's, how to spell *water*. The spice dealer calls out that he prefers to learn to write *customs form*. No, the letters come first! the teacher cries.

A few of them ask him to go through the letters more quickly; they lie down and commission their pals to wake them up when the letters are done. The farmer takes out his tobacco pouch and rolls himself a cigarette. The teacher won't let him smoke and tells him to wait until the break. The farmer walks up to the front of the room, takes the bell, and rings for the break. The teacher goes wild, screaming at the farmer to stand with his face to the wall. But the farmer leaves the room, and as he leaves, the greengrocer asks him to tell his donkey, waiting outside, to be patient a while longer.

The next evening only half as many people come. An eager porter is proud of having done his homework. Demanding recognition, he shows his notebook to the teacher, who makes a face because the porter has not kept within the lines. Sadly the porter replies, "It's not my fault. I write on the back of my trusty old donkey. The streets are full of potholes. The government plugs up one only to tear open another." Since he can write, the teacher ought to complain to the government about the holes.

When the butcher starts to laugh, the teacher tries to rap some manners into him with his ruler. But the butcher shatters the ruler and calls on his pals to strike. They all leave, and the teacher swears at them, calling them barbarians.

Our class split its sides with laughter. Mr. Katib praised Mahmud for his incisive wit. Nobody can write as amusingly as my friend.

November 16 — My father is happy that my poems pleased Mr. Katib. He said I take after him; he also wrote verse when he was a boy. After supper he even wanted to hear the poems. My mother yawned, and when he reproached her for this, she said she had to get up early or her dirty laundry would write a poem for her.

November 17 — The new history teacher has arrived. A funny sort of guy, all he ever wants to hear from us is dates. Right after getting acquainted, he wanted to test our knowledge. When was Napoleon born; when did Caesar die; when was this emperor appointed and that emperor deposed? After a while, he had us so far afield we scarcely knew when Syria had become independent.

Dates, dates, dates! What is all this? I don't think I'm going to make real contact with this teacher. Mahmud says this drillmaster must have been trained by a midwife or else at a funerary institute.

Sometimes, unfortunately, I have to admit that my father is right. What we're learning from this guy is sheer nonsense.

November 19 — For a brief moment Nadia stood by her door and smiled at me.

November 21 — Today Mr. Katib surprised me in the schoolyard. "Have you sent your poems to a publishing house?" he asked. I was speechless. Publishing house? That meant very little to me. Mr. Katib explained that writers send their stories and poems to publishing houses in order to bring their work to the public. He even gave me the name and address of a publisher. I'm supposed to send him a few of my poems, especially the two I recited in class. He's really serious. I'm a poet!

November 22 — I began my letter to the publisher three times, but each time it got too long. Mr. Katib said it should be brief and to the point. How can I describe in so few words why I write poems? I threw Leila out of the room three times because she wanted to touch the letter with her greasy fingers. She is so pigheaded today.

Now my letter is finally done. I wrote that I was enclosing seventeen poems I had already shown to my teacher. I may be very young, but the publisher should take into consideration that many of our poets started out young—just think of Jarir, the greatest poet of the Umayyad period. I also mentioned my uncle, the best poet in our neighborhood. Then I explained that although it might seem crazy to have a tree fly away, my teacher says that poems without madness are mere sermons. I also wrote I had composed all the poems by myself, without cribbing anything. He can check this himself. My mother can't even read, and though my father loves poetry, he never writes.

I hope the publisher will read the poems. If he prints them, I will light two candles for the Blessed Virgin. My mother doesn't understand what a publishing house is, so my father tried to explain to her. But to me he said the stamps on my envelope were a waste of money. Do I think the publisher has nothing better to do than answer the letter of a baker's son?

November 25 — I have not slept well for two days. All night I lie awake brooding about the publisher. Whatever will he think? Perhaps I should have written that I was seventeen. Or perhaps I should have copied my poems more neatly, on more expensive paper. What will he say when he reads that I am the son of a baker?

Yesterday I thought about paying him a visit myself.

The publishing house is in the New City, in central Damascus. What would I say? Maybe: "I just happened to be in the neighborhood and would like to speak to the publisher." The doorman will ask: "Whom shall I say is calling?" Oh, God, if only I were somewhat bigger and had finer trousers. There's really nothing to be done about the old ones. Still, my poems are good.

I am trying to imagine what a publisher looks like. Tall, thin, with graying temples and horn-rimmed glasses? Will he laugh when he reads my work? The poem "Dream on a Sack of Flour" will surprise him. I wrote him that I first scrawled that poem on the edge of an outdated newspaper since there was no better paper in the bakery.

November 27 — I had just made myself a cheese sandwich and sat down on the steps in front of our door when the madman approached me. His sparrow flew to a nearby balcony, as if it knew the madman wanted to sit down with me. Which he then did. He gazed at my sandwich and said, "Cheese!"

I divided it in half, and he ate slowly and deliberately and began to talk, until that idiot Georg kicked him as he passed by. The madman cowered and covered his head with his arms. The cheese flew somewhere nearby. I was so angry at Georg I could have strangled him. I caressed the madman, took the bare bread out of his cramped fingers, and gave him my portion. He gradually settled down and again began to whisper. I didn't understand much. Now and then I could pick out a word in Arabic, but all the rest were incomprehensible sounds.

"Say that again!" I asked and listened intently, but all I could understand was "Orient . . . color . . . rainbow . . ." and nothing more. Then he said quite clearly,

"Paper," and took a bite of the sandwich. I stood up. Georg was standing some distance away, smiling his repulsively conciliatory smile, as he always does after some obnoxious act. I threatened to beat him up if he so much as touched the man one more time. I brought the madman paper and a pencil, and he laughed, happy as a child. He rubbed his palms, took the pencil, and made a few signs. What strange writing. One sentence was in Arabic letters, followed by roman letters, but the words were neither French nor English. Then the word *Orient* in Arabic, then again a strange script, and on and on.

"Read!" he said, and smiled as he left. His Arabic script is so beautiful, almost like that in a book.

In the evening I showed the page to my father. He looked at it a long time. "This is Hebrew. This is Turkish, this Persian, and this Greek. But I can't read it." What could this man possibly have written?

November 28 — Mr. Katib asked Mahmud if he knew anyone who could type up his play; Mr. Katib wanted to send it to the radio. Mahmud didn't know anyone, so we asked if I might transcribe it in my good handwriting.

"No," Mr. Katib said. "People who work for the radio don't like handwritten texts." He decided to type Mahmud's play himself. What a great guy!

November 30 — Now the play looks splendid, typed up to look like a book. Mr. Katib attached a front page with Mahmud's name and the title: *The Letters of the Alphabet—A Radio Play*. The next page was a list of all the characters. Sometimes there were things in brackets, which had not been in the text before. Mr. Katib explained that he had indicated sounds and place descriptions; this was important so that listeners could get an idea of the atmosphere and the mood of the characters; after all, they would not be able to see them.

Mahmud is supposed to write a letter to a man by the name of Ahmad Malas; the address is quite simple: Syrian Radio, Damascus, Radio Play Department. This afternoon we sat and put together a letter. Mahmud was so very uneasy that he immediately ran to the post office.

December 1 — A Greek auto mechanic lives in our neighborhood. He laughs a lot and drinks even more, but he fixes cars splendidly and thus is always busy. I went to his workshop and showed him the madman's piece of paper.

He looked at it with his puffy eyes and laughed. "Only this one sentence on top is Greek, and this word down here. It is written in a very beautiful hand." He translated these segments for me, and I wrote down what he said in pencil. "Now listen, my boy, this is Italian, and next to it is Spanish. When you have solved the riddle, I want to know what the whole text means, too."

December 2 — Two blocks down there are a lot of Shi-'ites. After asking several questions, I made the acquaintance of a spice dealer of Persian descent. He translated the three passages that were written in Persian and said he did not think the man was crazy.

December 3 — Today Jakob, the greengrocer, translated the Hebrew words in the text for me. He told me that an old Spaniard lived near Thomas Gate and made violins.

December 4 — Was at the Spaniard's. Incredibly old! But super elegant. A fine man. He would not let me leave until he had shown me his best instrument, an old violin. He was surprised to hear the page came not from a teacher but from the madman. He also told me where I could find an Italian man, a pastrycook.

December 5 — I've lost the bet! Once again I'm a luckless person. Oh, well, it was only for a glass of orange juice. I bet Josef I could go to confession and come out without any penance. Josef said that Jesus himself could not go to see strict Father Johann and come out without an Our Father or at least an act of contrition.

No sooner said than done. I went in, knelt down, and before I could catch my breath, the priest asked, "What sins have we committed since last time, my son?"

"Last Saturday I made confession and have not sinned this week," I answered in a pious voice.

"This cannot be, my son. Gather your thoughts. Think of the Ten Commandments! Haven't you cursed?"

"No," I answered in a calm voice, because we do not regard such mild swearing as "Kiss my ass!" and "You dog" as sins. The first is an invitation and the second is one of God's creatures.

"Haven't you desired something that doesn't belong to you?"

"No," I said with a calm soul, because I love Nadia alone.

"Now think, my son! Haven't you lied at all?"

"No, not this week," I murmured with an uneasy feeling, since he was not letting me go.

"That is not possible. That is arrogance. Pray, my boy, that you will be able to receive humility in your heart once again. One Our Father and one act of contrition!"

December 6 — The pastrycook was not at home, but his wife also knows Italian, since she often goes to Italy to visit her in-laws. She translated the three Italian words and read everything that had been translated up to that point.

My father wanted to know whether I'd made anything out of the text yet (funny that this interests him, too). He looked at the page and said the script second from the last could only be Assyrian. He told me that two Kurdish families live on a side street. I should go to the little church nearby and ask a priest about it.

December 7 — Both the Kurdish families and the priest helped me out. The text is complete. The madman is a wise man! Here is his story:

Once upon a time, in a shady courtyard in the Orient, there lived a bird. Around its neck was a heavy, jewel-encrusted ring. The bird felt safe in its marble courtyard, enjoying the flowers' scent and joyfully listening to the plashing of the little fountain. When the master of the house had visitors, one of them would say, "Oh, what a lovely green bird!"

Another would contradict him, "Lovely, yes, but it's not green; it's brown. Look more closely."

"But my good sirs," a third would declare, "anyone who has eyes in his head can see the bird is blue!"

Even if the guests never agreed on the bird's color, all of them were enthralled by the beauty of the ring.

Autumn came. The leaves of the shade trees withered and fell, and the bird could see open sky. One day it caught sight of a flock heading south. It wanted to follow, but the heavy ring kept it earthbound. Day after day the cold intensified, and the little bird shivered and felt the bitterness of captivity.

At twilight on the seventh day, with a powerful jerk,

the bird wrenched itself free from the clinch of the heavy ring, which left a deep wound on its neck. Bleeding profusely, the liberated bird fluttered through the wide heavens. Over seas, deserts, mountains and valleys it flew, discerning the beauty of the world. It learned to outwit buzzards and snakes and to live with danger.

On the thirty-first day it reached the huge bird colony in the south and was astonished by the joyous reception of its fellow birds. An owl explained, "The coming of the rainbow bird means health and happiness for us all." Only now did the bird become aware of the multiplicity of the colors of its own feathers.

The rainbow bird lived a long life and flew all the way around the world. Whenever it saw a ring, however, the deep scar on its neck throbbed. . . .

Tomorrow, as promised, I will go round to all my new friends and take them the translation. This, I think, is the gift the madman wanted to give me. Now I know how many people of different nationalities live together here.

December 8 — After dinner my father wanted to hear some music. He turned on the radio, but instead of music, the voice of an Islamic scholar blared from the speaker. Unlike Uncle Salim, my father listens to everything about religion. I wasn't really paying attention, but suddenly my father began to curse the man who was speaking, who apparently said that Christians had no real religion and only imagined they followed a son of God.

"He talks as if the Christians in this country were deaf or couldn't understand Arabic. The devil take him! He's no authority; he's an idiot who's been loosed on us."

December 9 — A bitter disappointment! I was longing to see the madman and was enormously happy when I spotted him with his sparrow today. I ran home and brought him my dessert, an orange and some bread with marmalade. He would neither sit down nor accept the bread; mute and anxious, he just stared at me. To his sparrow he said:

> *Fly, bird, fly,*
> *the barbarians are coming.*
> *Fly to the clouds,*
> *where I've built a nest for you.*
> *Fly, fly away and take my sorrow with you.*
> *My joy will frighten the barbarians.*

I tried to talk to him about the story, but he seemed not to understand and kept repeating, "Fly, bird, fly!"

P.S.: Mahmud received an invitation from the editor at Syrian Radio. I thought he was joking, but the letter actually was signed by A. Malas. I am still waiting for a reply from the publisher.

December 11 — Mahmud went to the radio station today. The editor, surprised he was so young, asked whether Mahmud's father was an author. Mahmud said his father could not even write. Nor did he need to in order to sell potatoes. The editor laughed and had tea brought for him. He said the play still needed a lot of revision, and when he was finished working on it, he would inform Mahmud.

Uncle Salim was in stitches over Mahmud's play. He said that once, when he was a coachman, he had to pass an examination to determine whether he knew all the new street names and traffic signs. He told the examiner that he really ought to test his horse, because he himself often slept while driving; his horse was the one that found the way. The examiner supposedly had a good laugh and gave Uncle Salim a high grade.

December 12 — I had a great time with my mother today. I pretended to be a journalist and she acted like a know-it-all. It's a pleasure to hear my mother speak High Arabic. Like a queen, she exclusively uses the we-form and infinitives.

"In your opinion, Mrs. Hanne, what is Syria lacking?" I asked her in the kitchen.

With a slight, affected cough and mincing footsteps, my mother approached the invisible microphone I held in my hand. "When we consider it, we find that Syria is lacking in cakes and fertilizer."

I could not help giggling. My mother is always playing the blasé, offended Majesty.

"Where are the servants to remove this dreadful journalist from our palace? We do not like journalists. Journalists do not laugh!"

She herself burst out laughing at the word *palace*, because there we were, sitting in our shabby kitchen. She is truly a sight for the gods when she arrogantly sticks her nose up in the air and, with raised eyebrows, disapprovingly gazes at the poor journalist. It's easy to have a tremendous amount of fun with my mother.

Nadia asked me about the publisher. I told her she shouldn't be so impatient. After all, a man in his position has a lot to do. Will he answer?

December 13 — Nabil pinned a paper tail on the English teacher. It looked funny on that clotheshorse.

Today my old man messed up a batch of pound cakes again. Now all day long we have to choke down this dry, burned stuff! He can't even sell them to the poor.

It's been raining for days. Still no answer from the publisher.

December 14 — Nadia's parents and her two brothers went to a party. I sneaked over to her house, and she showed me where she sleeps. I stretched out beside her on the little bed. She lay quite close to me, and I could smell the perfume in her hair. She knows that jasmine is my favorite flower.

December 15 — Hooray!!! The publisher answered today. His letter was friendly, and he thought my poems were good. Great! He wants to print five of them in an anthology of young poets; the rest weren't bad either. I am to send him a photo and visit him sometime, whenever I choose.

I'm going to appear in a book as a poet! Blessed Mary, I will light two candles in church for you tomorrow.

My father was bowled over. For the first time in months, he embraced me. He was very proud of me; he had tears in his eyes when he said that at such moments he knew he had not lived in vain. I'm supposed to get a new pair of trousers and take a bath before I go to see the publisher; my dad has even given my mother money for these things. She, however, no longer understands the ways of the world. She thought poets were always starving, and now her little poet is about to get new trousers. Then she began to wail: If only her sainted father could have experienced this, how happy and proud he would have been. Then my father grew stern and told her to stop talking about the dead. After all, did anyone give a thought to *his* old father?

"Now we'll celebrate," he said and then made coffee for my mother and me.

"What a father you have; how very much he loves you," my mother sobbed, wiping the tears from her cheeks with the hem of her apron. Then she pulled herself together, went to wash her face, and we all had coffee. I am to go to Basil, the photographer, to have a good photo taken.

And for all this I have to thank that wonderful man, Mr. Katib!

December 17 — Never has it rained so much as in the past few weeks. The sky seems to have decided to answer the prayers of all the farmers at the same time. This blessing for the farmers is a curse for Damascus. The rain washes the clay out of the roofs and walls and makes the streets muddy. The sewer system in our old part of town isn't functioning, and last night when the temperature went below freezing, many water pipes burst.

Mahmud and Nadia are very proud that my poems are going to appear in a book.

December 18 — A bitter defeat for my mother! For weeks she has been bugging me to sing in the church choir. For her sake, I went there today. She gave me two oranges as a reward, and this annoyed my sister. Now she, too, wants to sing in a choir, provided she gets a couple of oranges for it.

We gathered in the churchyard at two o'clock. Father Georgios, who is responsible for the choir, came for us. First he wanted to test the newcomers, to see if any of our voices might already be breaking. We had to line up by size, and since I'm already 165 centimeters tall, I stood all the way in the back. We had to sing a couple of Kyrie Eleisons, but each time we did, Father Georgios looked extremely irritated.

"Someone is droning," he said. He singled out fat Georg in the first row, whispered something to him, and the fatso slinked out with lowered head. Now we had to resume singing, but still he was not content.

"Who is it that's droning then?" he asked disapprovingly.

We all looked at one another and shrugged our shoulders. Then he divided us into three small groups. Mine was the one that had the drone. I tried to sing as lightly and finely as possible.

Father Georgios nodded his head meaningfully. He came up to me, patted me on the shoulder, and said, "No offense, my son, but your voice is far too deep." Oh, well, bad luck.

When I came out, Georg was still loafing around outside the door. He laughed at me disgustingly. "Such idiotic croaking," he said, "I sang wrong on purpose the whole time." All the way home he screeched into my ears.

When I got home, I was astonished at how many neighbor women were having coffee with my mother. She had rashly told everyone that the priest had personally invited me to join the choir. When she saw me standing in the doorway so early, she looked dumbfounded. When I told her the priest had kicked me out, my mother suddenly ranted and raged against the priest. The other women hypocritically tried to console her—only my mother would hear no more and grumbled, "What does that old crow know about singing?"

December 23 — Owing to the incessant rain, the clay roofs have become sodden; water seeps through and drops into all our apartments. Our ceiling leaks in several places. It's not so bad in my parents' room, but in the living room, where Leila and I sleep, it's nerve-racking. Like everyone else, my father is afraid to go up on the slippery roof to plug up the holes. So there's nothing for my mother to do but set pots and buckets everywhere. I can't sleep. I feel like I'm inside a limestone cave. Drip, drip, drip. It drives me up the wall!

P.S.: Mahmud laughed himself half to death when I told him about the choir. He wants to hear the story over and over again!

December 25 — Christmas. Today we had a fabulous meal. My mother really surpassed herself; my father brought home a bottle of red wine, which we all emptied. Even Leila had a little glass.

The
Second
Year

January 7 — Some of my schoolmates are ill. This weather is really the pits! Leila and Uncle Salim also have colds.

Today Leila had a fever attack. She sat up in bed and began to sing. Raising her right hand, she swayed back and forth, as if she wanted to dance. I laughed, which my mother found absolutely appalling. She threw me out of the room.

Once Leila had calmed down and fallen asleep, my mother reproached me: "A person can go mad from such a high fever, and there you are, laughing like an idiot!"
P.S.: I went to the publisher, but he wasn't in. He'll be back on the tenth of January.

January 10 — Today I went to the publishing house. Was I ever trembling; I scarcely made a sound as I stood before the publisher, but there was no reason to have gotten so worked up. He is a little bald man with rather fat fingers; he smokes like a chimney and coughs non-stop. He was incredibly friendly. My fear that he might consider me too young vanished with his first few remarks.

He treated me like an adult, telling me about his problems and about the wonderful books he had already brought out and the others he still plans to. I was surprised to learn he doesn't own a printing shop. He gave me a beautiful book of poems, then talked about my poems, which he intends to publish in the summer. He read them aloud and said he liked the one about the flying tree best and that he also plans to place it first in the book. I was so happy I could have hugged him!

I walked all the way home; I wanted to be alone. I looked at the bare trees. It was sunny and cold, and I saw myself, hand in hand with Nadia, reading poems in front of a huge audience.

January 12 — The radio drones on and on about war. My father hates war; he says one person has no right to take another's life. Lately I've been having bad dreams and growing more and more fearful.

January 13 — Our religion class was great fun today.

"Why does Jesus have blond hair and blue eyes in all the pictures?" Josef asked the priest.

The priest jabbered something about Jesus radiating peace.

But cheeky Josef would not buy this explanation. "Was Jesus born in Palestine or wasn't he? Palestinians and Jews have dark eyes and hair, and they look peaceful, too."

The priest became all the more enmeshed in his own web of prattle. But Josef had only asked the first question so he could push on to the real issue: "And why haven't we had a Palestinian pope yet? Eh? Or an African pope?"

This threw the priest completely off balance, and he

ordered Josef to write out the act of contrition ten times as punishment. What a weak response.

During recess I told Josef how much I want to become a journalist. He laughed at me. "A journalist lives on questions, but here you get acts of contrition for asking. I want to be an officer. An officer never asks; he gives and carries out orders."

I should have picked some other time to tell him.

P.S.: Leila is well again and just as impudent as ever.

January 15 — Uncle Salim has also recovered. I'm so glad!

It was warm out; he emerged from his room to enjoy the sun in silence. Bundled up in a quilt, he sat quietly and smiled at me as I chased all the children out of the courtyard so he would have some peace.

January 16 — We didn't know whether to laugh or cry. When we were coming back from school, Uncle Salim was already waiting for us at the front door. His voice was far from cheerful as he told Mahmud that his radio play had been broadcast at eleven in the morning. Mahmud immediately asked if they had mentioned he was the author. Uncle Salim hesitated—maybe he had missed it. But he could not put Mahmud off with that answer for long. Then he admitted that Ahmad Malas had been named as the author.

I just don't get it. There must have been a misunderstanding. We'll see; tomorrow afternoon the broadcast will be repeated. Maybe Uncle Salim didn't hear right.

January 17 — What a dirty trick! Mahmud has been wailing. The shameless script editor passes himself off as the author of the play and doesn't say a word about

Mahmud. Certainly Mr. Katib also heard it today. We told him when it would be broadcast. It just can't be true!

And what if the publisher were to steal my poems and pass them off as his own son's?

January 18 — Mr. Katib is appalled. He wrote a furious letter to the editor, informing him that over fifty students were witness to his outrageous act of theft. He demanded a correction and an apology. Mahmud mailed the letter, but he doubted it would have any effect. Mr. Katib reassured me, however, that he knew the publisher, and that man would never do such a disgraceful thing. All he knew about the editor was that he was always encouraging young authors to send him their plays.

January 20 — I really enjoy writing in my journal. Today my parents and Leila went to visit a sick uncle. I made myself some tea and sat down by the window. Nadia briefly looked out of the door to her house and waved, and I sent her a "flying kiss."

Distance was the mother of this invention. My lips make a kiss just as if she were there; then I pluck the kiss out of the air like a jasmine blossom. This must be done very slowly. Then I lay the kiss on the palm of my hand and gently blow it in her direction. Momentarily, she catches it and places it wherever she likes—sometimes on her cheek, her lips, or even under her blouse.

Now, after the flying kiss Nadia put to her lips, I write a little and leaf through my journal. There's already quite a lot inside it, and this spurs me to keep writing. Otherwise I would never know where something happened and who said what to whom.

January 22, afternoon — Yesterday we decided to punish the script editor. Josef got the idea to execute judgment in the name of the Black Hand.

"But we have disbanded!" I said.

"Justice demands it, my little one," Josef answered in the deep voice of a grandfather.

We laughed, and then we talked about what we would do. We decided on a couple of things. In the middle of the night Josef will write with red paint on the wall opposite the radio station: *All script editors have hollow heads! Give them your ideas! The Black Hand.*

Mahmud and I will cover Josef. And in a couple of days' time, he and I will attend to the editor while Josef is on the lookout.

January 24 — First thing this morning we had to take a look at what had become of the writing on the wall. It seemed to amuse a few passersby.

"Of course," one of them said to his wife. "I noticed that myself long ago; that's why I don't listen to the radio anymore."

A wise guy called out, "Then they should go begging on the street and gather a few fresh ideas!"

Everybody laughed. It wasn't long before an official from the radio station came with a bucket of paint and rapidly eliminated our message.

Mahmud felt great. He laughed at the bureaucrat.

January 25 — I was going to take care of the editor, during which time Mahmud would see to his car. We sneaked into the radio station's parking lot and lay in wait. Finally he arrived—he's a small man who hops nervously when he walks! Mahmud slit all four tires and taped the following message on his windshield: *Best regards from the Black Hand.* I drew my slingshot and fired a packet of red paint at him. It hit him with such force, he was nearly scared to death. As if deranged, he began to scream, "I've been wounded! Blood! I've been wounded!" We ran as fast as we could.

P.S.: Josef couldn't join us because he had to do his chores. Odd, usually he shirks them.

January 27 — Now I'm writing lots of poems, especially about Nadia, whom I love very much.

Tuesday — Shit! Since yesterday I've been working full-time in the bakery. This winter many people have returned to their villages to till their fields, or else they're emigrating to the Gulf states, or God only knows where they've fled to. My father couldn't find any workers. I've neglected my math homework. Our math teacher is all right, but he's very strict, and through Mahmud he let me know that I have at most two weeks in which to make up the work; otherwise I'll be put on warning. Our Arabic teacher also asked about me today.

Funny. Both yesterday and today my old man gave me three pounds after work. Because I'm entitled, he said.

February 7 — My seventh day in the bakery! Today, at lunchtime, I had to deliver bread to the restaurant near school. The students were just then storming out of the building. A few of the biggest imbeciles in my class gathered around my cart and began to mock me. "Bakery errand boy," jeered the goldsmith's son. What a mean thing to say! The others snickered. I would like to have thrashed them all. Then they started to paw the bread, trying to tear chunks off. Mahmud came to my aid, and we succeeded in fending them off for a while. There would have been quite a stink if the restaurant owner had gotten partially eaten bread. But the idiots refused to understand this, and a real brawl ensued. Mahmud and I against the two loudmouths, the dentist's sons. We showed them what we're made of; they ran off with their tails between their legs.

My old man cursed me even more because I came back so late and so filthy. I didn't say a word about the fistfight. I hope he finds a worker soon!

Monday — Damn it! The biology exam has come and gone. I've already been put on warning in history and math. My father has declined to answer the principal's letter. He said the principal could wait a few days; I'd soon be back in school. Every day he gives me three pounds. But I don't want the stupid money; I want to be back in school!

Nadia says I've become very aggressive lately. What does she know? I told her to work in the bakery just one day and see how she feels then.

February 14 — I can't stand it! Now I have learned the truth. How can he be so mean? My old man doesn't want me to continue in school. What a cheat! He's just been putting me off the whole time!

Mr. Katib visited my father today, to try to persuade him that he'd be making a mistake if he took me out of school. My father acted as if the teacher did not exist. But Mr. Katib didn't give up so easily; he was adamant. He waited politely until my father had taken care of his customers; then he began to press my father again. My father said it was no concern of Mr. Katib's; after all, I am his son, and he can make of me whatever he chooses to. I was so ashamed I wanted to sink into the ground.

Mr. Katib remained entirely calm and went on talking. My old man got louder and louder. He has no fear of teachers or officials. He said school no longer interested me and asked me in a loud and angry voice whether this wasn't true. Totally dismayed, I could not utter a word and began to howl. When Mr. Katib spoke of parental duty, my father became really nasty. He reviled the teacher and the school. He knew very well that school was compulsory only through the fifth grade; the teacher shouldn't think he was stupid just because he was a baker. Mr. Katib tried to explain to my father that he had meant a different duty, but my father was pissed off and pushed him out the door. He so truly enjoyed his victory over the teacher that he flaunted it all afternoon in front of his employees!

I'm not speaking to him any longer. I feel paralyzed. At some point he tried again to explain the difficult situation he was in and that he, too, would have liked to stay in school. But he had simply been stuck in the bakery. He said he understood my anger, but soon I would have far more pocket money than any of my friends. He would even give me four pounds a day, which would come to over a thousand a year.

When he had concluded his litany, I asked him why we were supposed to be bakers and nothing else. Surprised, he looked at me and declared this was our fate.

Not mine! I don't want it to be! I want to go on in school and become a journalist!

My mother tried to soothe me. Things would soon be better; I shouldn't take my father's words so seriously. It's just one of those bad times.

I don't want to speak to him ever again.

February 16 — Nadia has changed; she's become so strange. And that horrid Josef—my so-called friend—has been giving her the eye. I think they're making fun of me. Mahmud says that a girl should not be ashamed of her boyfriend, even if he is a baker. Mahmud's mother was disowned because she loved his father. She comes from a very wealthy family and ran off with Mahmud's father instead of marrying her cousin. To this day she lives with her husband in poverty because she loves him. Mahmud says it's better to forget Nadia.

But I can't! I love her!

February 17 — I told Mahmud about the fight with my old man. Laughing, he said that all fathers are the same. He would like to see the day when fathers exchange places with their sons, if only for a few hours. Would they be in for a surprise; he thinks many fathers would freak out if they could read their sons' minds. I admire Mahmud because he can laugh about everything—himself, his father, our teachers, even though he really doesn't have much to laugh about.

February 19 — Today I told Uncle Salim my secret. I really can't stand it any longer. I'm going to run away. He asked if I had considered this carefully. I told him I had saved up nearly two hundred Syrian pounds. I have to get away from here. He looked at me sadly and said he wanted to speak to my father one more time. Maybe, after all, he might be open to discussion. I don't want to grow old in the bakery and one day say to my son: You are supposed to become what I have been.

February 26, 11 P.M. — Neither Uncle Salim nor my mother can convince my old man I should go to school. We quarrel every day. Today I threatened to run away if he won't let me go back. He just laughed and asked where I would go. I don't care where, as long as I don't have to work in the bakery.

My mother wept for a long time; Nadia blanched when I confided in her and said she felt sick; nonetheless, I want to get away. Tonight, when everyone is asleep, I will bundle up my clothes. I will also take my notebook of poems, the photo of Nadia, and my journal. If I don't get out of here, it will be the end of me.

I will set out for Aleppo, the biggest city of the north, far from my father's hand and my mother's tears. I don't want to cry anymore. I want to laugh and live as I like. Somewhere in Aleppo I'll find a room I can rent for twenty pounds a month. As soon as I get there, I'll try to find a newspaper that will have me. I'll clean the floors, make tea for the journalists, deliver mail. All they need to do is show me how to become a good journalist. And if I can't earn my living that way, I will get some kind of work during the day, and at night maybe I'll write about all the things I've heard people discussing.

I want to make a clean break. These are the last lines from Damascus. Nothing holds me here any longer.

February 27 — Last night I crept downstairs, intending to flee, and there on the bottom step, in the dark, sat Uncle Salim. Did I ever get a scare!

"Were you going to leave without saying good-bye to your friend?" he whispered and took me into his arms. I started to bawl.

"Let me go, I want to leave," I begged him. But he insisted on having tea first—then I could go to Alaska or anywhere I liked. I gave in, and we went to his tiny kitchen. He made the tea in silence and carried it into his room; I followed him.

"You will be a good journalist," he said, giving me some tea. "Yes, and I know you will write about me and my silly stories. I know that in my heart."

"But the bakery is killing me," I protested.

"That's a fact. It is bad. In the past I envied bakers, but since you and I have become friends, I pity them." He nodded and said nothing for a time. "But what will be different in Aleppo? Can you tell me that? Not that I have any great love for Damascus. Coachmen, like beggars, have no place they call home. No, I don't like Damascus, but how will Aleppo be different? If you want to run away, emigrate to Saudi Arabia. You can earn a lot more money there. Aleppo? It's just like here, a pile of manure."

"But I'm only fifteen, and they won't let me out of the country!"

"That's true. What a stupid government!" He poured more tea, stroked my hair. "And have you given any thought to finding me a friend as good as you to take your place before you leave? Eh? I have two children and thirteen grandchildren, none of whom I'm as fond of as you, and what do you do? You go off and leave me alone. I hate bakeries!"

"I will never forget you. I'll write to you," I promised and started to wail again, for at this moment I felt both my best friend's sorrow and my own.

"You'll write, but I can't read! I'll have to go around asking people to read your letters to me. And I couldn't really ask them to write back, because, after all, that wouldn't be the same as talking to you."

"But I'm suffocating here!"

"You're suffocating because you have given up. Salim never gave up! When I was freezing, starving, and had to live like a dog in the mountains because I did not want to go into the army, I, too, considered ending the shame and doing my military service. But I held out and brooded over how to fight my way through. In the spring a shepherd came along, gave me something to eat, and invited me to work for him. He got me false papers, and so for five years my name was not Salim but Mustafa, and my life as a shepherd wasn't so bad. Many of my friends, who laughed at me at first, later regretted it, for in 1914 the Great War broke out, and many of them were wounded, missing, or killed. But the shepherds never went hungry. Give some more thought to how you can get out of the bakery without running away. You've got brains. You know your way around Damascus. Let yourself get an idea, and perhaps we can cook up some scheme together. Salim is always good for a plan. And you, my friend, will be a good journalist. Of that I'm sure."

I was quiet a long time, and Uncle Salim went on talking. Of course, I didn't believe it would work out, but when he said, "Just try it for half a year. Today is February 26. Six months from now, we'll sit down together again, and if things haven't improved, I will carry your bag to the bus station, so you can go wherever you like. Is that asking too much? Half a year!"

All right, then, I will try to find a solution here in Damascus. I can always run off after six months have gone by.

"Do you promise?" Uncle Salim asked.

"I promise!" I said and crept back into bed.

March 1 — "Then write me about what's wrong," I implored Nadia when she passed our house on her way to get milk.

"Why should I? So you can show it off?" she said coldly. I just don't understand. She must be crazy.

March 4 — In the early morning my soul throbs at the sight of students, hair just combed, on their way to school. Sometimes my old man notices, strokes my hair, and for a while is very nice to me. Once he even wept and said, "You're more clever than all those students. I know what kind of son I brought into the world." Another time he said, "All people are born the same, naked, but after only three breaths they are different."

Sometimes I really feel compassion for him. I don't think my father wanted to become a baker either.

March 6 — Today I learned that Uncle Salim slept on the stairs for more than that one night. He was on guard for a whole week. He understood I truly did want to escape. What a fabulous friend!

March 8 — Today I convinced my old man that I can best help him by delivering bread. Well-to-do customers, who can afford to pay a bit more, get fresh bread delivered to their homes. I won't need to work in the heat and a haze of flour and can win new customers for my father's business. At first he would not agree to this, but after a week of arguments, he wanted his peace and came around.

It's hard work. I have to carry a basket containing fifteen kilos of bread and run up and down stairs—some of these people live five floors up. Altogether I deliver sixty kilos per day. There are four rounds; I'm done by noon. Some of the customers are stupid; others are nice and give me a piaster or an apple. What rankles, however, is that now I have to deliver bread to a few of my former classmates, and they laugh at me. Nonetheless, Uncle Salim says I have already taken a giant step forward. I have escaped further instruction at the dough machine or the oven. He thinks it's only a matter of time before my father can do without me. I'm not so sure; perhaps Uncle Salim is overly optimistic.

March 9 — "Stop telling me about your love," Nadia snapped at me when I whispered a few terms of endearment to her. Then she simply ran past me into her house. How curious! Whatever does she think of me?

March 20 — I have acquired many new customers. Now, by early afternoon, I've delivered one hundred and twenty kilos of bread. My old man is very pleased because his bakery has never had so much business before. I don't like the work, but most of my time is my own. I read a lot and write poems.

Today I wrote my first article, about a woman I have been delivering bread to for a week. Sometimes she's as happy as a child, and sometimes she's so sad that she cries. When I read my work to Uncle Salim, he said, "But a journalist must also know the reason the woman is the way she is."

March 21 — Today I selected an especially good loaf of bread for the woman. She looked downcast but invited me to have some tea. Her apartment is lovely. After a while, she became talkative, and I got to hear her story.

Her name is Mariam, and she comes from a village in the north. She was very much in love with her childhood sweetheart, but her parents wanted to give her away to a rich old geezer, and so Mariam and her boyfriend fled to Damascus. They married and lived together very happily. Then her husband lost his job, and though he searched long and hard, he could not find work. Finally he learned of a job in Kuwait and accepted it without delay, even though he could not take his wife with him. He was gone for five years, coming back only two weeks each year. Now he has returned for good—a rich man. He has a big business and is very content, but being abroad changed him. He is never any fun; he never caresses her; he bestows all his love on his business. She lacks neither food nor clothing, but she feels very lonesome.

This is the cause of her sadness. Yet, despite all my questions, I don't know why she is sometimes cheerful. Mariam denied that she ever is. I still want to find out why!

March 23 — Today, once again, I have grave doubts whether my decision to remain here was right. Two of the dumbest kids in my class threw stones at me. The sissies knew I could not leave my basket unattended to pursue them. One stone hit my ear, and it bled.

And Nadia has changed. She avoids me. I haven't been able to speak to her for days. Josef said she disparagingly called me a baker boy. Somehow or other I have the feeling that Josef enjoyed making a fool of me.

March 27 — "Greetings!" I said, when I saw Nadia with her eldest brother on the street.

"Greetings!" he answered and was about to give me his hand when Nadia looked away and kept walking, as if she didn't recognize me. I felt a stabbing pain in my heart and completely forgot about her brother.

March 30 — Uncle Salim changed barbers today. He came home with short hair and several facial wounds, but he laughed and swore he wouldn't go anywhere else. I was amazed he had left the best barber on our street and sought out a butcher who cut him up like a piece of meat.

"For twenty years good old Sami has cut my hair, but from day to day he says less and less. I've had enough of his silence. A barber should tell stories better than the radio. Sami regards each story as a loss; it's as if he counts up every word. And he bores me with his "Yes, yes, you don't say," while he doesn't listen to anything you are telling him. Sami may have a lot of clients, but today I went looking for a new barber and found one at Thomas Gate.

"This barber has an assistant, and since I was new, he left me to the boy while he himself attended to his regular customers. The lad has quite a mouth but was born with bumbling hands. They're like two big shovels and would be better off on a farmer than a barber. He dragged the shears through my hair as if my head were an overgrown meadow. We both laughed when I told him my haircut looked so ridiculous, the army would be glad to take me. Chattering away, he soaped up my beard, and as he started to shave me, he began to tell the story of the witless king and his cunning wife. Again I laughed because he told the story so well, which resulted in a cut on my cheek. It hurt like hell! He asked a thousand pardons and tried to stem the flow of blood. In the mirror I saw the boss raise an arm to box his assistant's ears. The sly fox pretended not to notice a thing, but at the last moment he stooped down, and I got the blow! The boss apologized, cursed at him, and went back to his own customer.

"The boy went on talking and cut me again, but it wasn't so bad. I said I felt like a sheep in his hands; he laughed, and the razor skidded along. It hurt and I cried out loud. This time the boss approached softly, ready to strike, and—because the assistant got out of the way just as craftily as before—his hand landed around my neck. He apologized many times for his clumsiness, and when his assistant wounded my right cheek again, I didn't cry out. When the assistant was finally done, I wanted to pay, but the embarrassed barber wouldn't take any money.

"'A free shave for two blows! I'll be back!' I said, and we all laughed."

Next Saturday I don't want to go back to my cousin's. He's not a good barber; all he ever talks about are his debts.

Saturday — What a crazy shop! The master barber is Armenian; his assistant comes from Persia. But the barber's grandparents came to Syria a long time ago.

Unlike my cousin's or Sami's posh establishments, this barbershop is an incredible mess. In one corner is a grinding wheel; in another, a big, dusty case filled with jars, lavender water, rose water, and jasmine water, as well as two large aquariums full of leeches. These worms look disgusting but are supposed to be very useful. Along one wall is a row of chairs and a splendid heap of magazines.

I sat down, greedily read the illustrated magazines, and laughed at the barber and his assistant. The boy would not stop kidding around, and the master did nothing but moan and wail.

When a woman approached the grinding wheel, the barber simply left his soaped-up client sitting there, took the woman's old knife, and slowly began to sharpen it. The man complained, but the barber suddenly seemed unable to understand Arabic, answering only in Armenian.

The best thing is that the haircut cost only half what it does at my beloved relative's. I got an ice cream out of it, too.

April 6 — "Let's go for a walk in the fields," I suggested to Nadia, when she smiled at me at the greengrocer's.

"It's all very well for you to talk," she said and ran off, as if I were a skunk. What in heaven's name is wrong with her? Does she love me or doesn't she?

April 11 — In all his life Uncle Salim never worked more than three days a week; three days he spent with his family, and on the seventh day he withdrew and reflected. He never became rich, nor did he ever live in dire want. Today he told me a lot about the wisdom of death, which only a few understand. "Every moment, my boy, Death tells us: Live! Live! Live!"

Today my old man had a bad day and was in a rotten mood in the evening. When Uncle Salim joined him for tea, my father made an effort to be more cheerful because he respects Uncle Salim and likes him so much.

But nobody can hide anything from our old neighbor. He may be nearsighted, but he can always see straight through you.

"Do as I do," he recommended to my father. "I sometimes had very bad days, too; nonetheless, I learned how to feel good at home afterward."

"How do I do that, Uncle?" my old man wanted to know.

"When you get to the house, stand outside the door and say to your troubles: 'Get off my shoulders, Troubles, get off!' Then go in, and the next morning on your way out, stand on the same spot and say: 'Troubles, you can get back on my shoulders now!' But you must not leave them behind on the doorstep, for then they will take their revenge."

My father laughed, stroked Uncle Salim's knee, and said, "But what if they come after me through the cracks in the door? What then?"

"Then call upon your friend Salim, and I'll come with my dagger, and you'll see, they'll cringe like dogs and slink away!"

We all laughed, and I seemed to feel the troubles disappearing.

April 15 — A tourist has settled in our neighborhood. He has a permit from the government, and according to Mahmud, he converted to Islam long ago. Unlike Robert, he is not much fun; he always has a look on his face that seems to say he's expecting an earthquake.

At first his Muslim neighbors admired him, praising his piety. But he is so strictly observant they are now fed up with him. He uses far too much water because he washes himself five times a day and his car once a day. Damascus is so dusty that his car instantly gets dirty again. That alone isn't so bad, but the vehicle has a magnetic attraction for us and for dogs, and we all piss on the tires. The enraged man wrote on four pieces of paper in red Arabic script, "Pissing forbidden!" and taped them inside the car windows. But children don't read while they pee. They just laugh!

April 18 — I wanted to see her badly. Mahmud suggested that I kick a soccer ball into the courtyard of her house. And so I shot the ball in a high arc over the wall, knocked on the door, and entered the house. Nadia, her mother, and both her brothers were sitting in the yard.

I asked about the ball. The elder of her brothers sneered, "Nadia! Give him the ball; it's behind the flowerpots." But Nadia didn't move a muscle. The younger of the two stood up, gave me the ball, and whispered, "She's been acting peculiar lately."

"Leave Nadia alone," his mother called to him, having heard him whisper.

Nadia really is acting strange. She didn't even say good-bye when I left. Mahmud grumbled about her.

April 26 — Two months have gone by; my customers are satisfied with me, and no other baker can take them away. My old man is slowly getting back on his feet. His debts are smaller and his bakery is flourishing. The work is not difficult. I can carry the baskets more easily, and the stairs no longer bother me. But the boredom! I read a lot, but I write little, except in my journal.

Uncle Salim gives me strength every single day. He insists on discussing my work. He gets angry along with me, and at times I even have to reassure him that the bakery is not always hell.

I only feel good at Mariam's. She never lets me leave

before I have had some tea or coffee. I like her a lot and think she likes me too. I still have not found out how she can sometimes be as happy and carefree as a child.

For more than a week Nadia has been in the village where her grandparents live. Why, I don't know.

April 28 — What a surprise! Mariam gave me a blue shirt today. However could she know that blue is my favorite color?

"It will look great on you with your white slacks," she said and kissed me on the cheek. Is she in love with me? Uncle Salim says love has nothing to do with age, but that I ought to take care her husband doesn't catch me.

Is he pulling my leg, or have I spiced up my stories about Mariam too much?

April 29 — Today I brought Mariam a cake. I told her about the profession I dream of. She laughed—I don't know why—and promised to help me. A neighbor of hers, named Habib, is a fine journalist. She will tell him about me. Tomorrow I am supposed to bring along a delectable sweet bread.

April 30 — Ha! It worked out! Mariam is fantastic! She actually accompanied me to the third floor and rang the bell. After a while, a man of about fifty opened the door, still in his pajamas. Yawning, he smiled and asked us in. "How elegant bakers have become," he said. I was wearing my white pants, my white tennis shoes, and the blue shirt Mariam gave me. The whole day my father had been griping about how I was dressed.

Habib took the bread and sniffed it. "Delicious! Mariam wasn't exaggerating!"

We had tea in a completely disorganized room. Mariam was happy as a child. As we were leaving, Habib asked if I could bring him half a kilo of the bread every day. Can I ever!

Friday — I knew Habib was free today. I selected the best bread for him. Extra crusty, the way he likes it. I brought it to him when I had finished one of my rounds and had an hour before starting on my noon round.

He invited me to have some tea; I sat in his living room while he made it. Books and newspapers were everywhere, especially French ones. His pants lay on a chair, and on a crowded little tabletop were a bottle of *arrack*, a big ashtray, and several glasses. Habib must have had guests the previous day.

A thick book by Kahlil Gibran was also lying around. I love this author dearly, but I only know a few of his works. I was leafing through the book when Habib brought the teapot in.

"Do you like Gibran?" he asked me.

"Naturally I like him. He loves children and understands them better than anyone."

"Do you know much about his tragic life?"

"Of course," I declared, although all I knew was that the best poet in Lebanon had to become famous abroad before his own country recognized him. He emigrated to America.

"You're not just bragging?" Habib asked somewhat suspiciously.

"No! Why should I? Shall I recite something for you?" I asked, sure of myself, because I knew two of his pieces by heart.

"Go ahead, my boy. It's always good to hear Gibran." I astonished Habib. "A baker boy treasures Gibran, and the editor in chief asks who he is," he said softly, as if to himself.

I told him I wanted to be a journalist and asked him to teach me something about his profession.

"Forget about it, my boy! I would rather be a baker; at least a baker knows he's doing something useful."

In some way I'm afraid of Habib. He's different from Uncle Salim. He is often extremely curt. I didn't dare smoke at his place, though I had cigarettes with me. Unlike Uncle Salim, he is embittered and angry about everything, although his anger can suddenly be transformed into explosive joy. He laughed at my dreams for the future. I was afraid he would not want to see me again, but as I was leaving, he gave me the book by Gibran. "Take it. I want to discuss it with you. But forget about newspapers!"

May 10 — Mahmud has also been taken out of school. His father doesn't want him there either; he cannot feed nine mouths by himself. "They bring children into the world and then they moan and groan," Mahmud cursed, for, just like me, he enjoyed going to school. Mahmud's fondest hope was to become a pilot and see the world. Poverty smothers our dreams even before we have finished dreaming them.

Now Mahmud is working in a café in the New City. Of those in our gang, only Josef is still in school. His mother wants him to be a doctor. She inherited some fields in the vicinity of the city, and each year their value increases; she saves everything for his studies. Josef a doctor! I would sooner let a butcher operate on me. Josef doesn't even know how to tell a heart from a kidney. He wants to be a military officer, which horrifies both us and his mother.

May 14 — I have grave doubts whether my decision to stay in Damascus was the right one. I tumbled down a flight of stairs this afternoon and scraped my left arm. It hurt like hell. And the people who live in that goddamned high-rise swiped the bread.

Josef said that pearls, hidden in their shells, need the wide sea, pure water, and the sun in order to grow. "Has a shell in the sewers of Damascus ever brought pearls into the world?" he asked sadly. Not meaning to, he grazed an open wound. The bakery is doing me in. What will become of me?

May 16 — I didn't know Uncle Salim could get so angry. Today he spent a long time preparing his water pipe, then made himself some tea, and sat in the courtyard in front of his door. Children were playing with a tennis ball. Uncle Salim admonished the children to let him smoke his pipe in peace for an hour, but the children of Abdu the truck driver went on playing.

Suddenly the ball hit the water pipe, which fell to the ground, luckily without shattering, but tobacco was strewn all over. Salim cursed the snot-nosed brats who deprived him of his pleasure. The children's father felt insulted. He offered Uncle Salim a pack of cigarettes and said he shouldn't make such a big deal over a pipe.

"You really ought to teach your children that I, too, have a right to one square meter in front of my door and to one hour of peace a day," Uncle Salim cried.

A wild fight ensued. The truck driver called Uncle Salim a conceited pasha. Uncle Salim went mad and cursed the man out. My father heard the argument and asked my mother to hurry and make a big pot of coffee. He rushed down in his pajamas and tried to talk to the truck driver and then to Uncle Salim. Both of them calmed down a little, and when my mother served the coffee, the dispute was forgotten. Abdu's wife brought Uncle Salim a splendidly decorated water pipe.

May 22 — Nadia is back! At last I have seen her again! And just now she secretly pressed a thick envelope into my hand, containing letters she wrote me during this whole difficult time. Feebleminded imbecile that I am, I doubted her love. I could kick myself! She loves me!!!

I have never read such beautiful, sad letters. Now I also know why she was acting so strangely. Her brother had seen us kissing and had told her father. The barbarian had hit her and locked her in her room, threatening to punish the whole family if she said a word to anyone. Nadia had to eat alone there; her father only unlocked her door in the evening so she could go to the toilet. Later he let her go out, but only with her two brothers following after her like dogs. They gave her such a fright, telling her that she should only know what Mahmud and Josef say about her, since I was always boasting about her to them. (This is not true; I have scarcely told the two of them anything about Nadia!) She doubted me and was so scared she got sick. Then her father sent her to her grandparents in the country, where she had peace and felt her love for me even more strongly. She wants to meet me, but her brothers won't leave her alone.

I have to be careful that nothing happens to Nadia.

May 23 — Uncle Salim is a very bad cook. He never really learned how, and he is far too proud to ask anyone's help. My mother and the other neighbor women are always thinking up new ways to see that the proud widower gets something good to eat.

"You understand a lot more about food than my husband. He says this has no taste; please try some of it and tell me your honest opinion."

"I burned my tongue drinking coffee. Just taste this little dish and tell me if anything's missing."

"Today, after fifteen years, I've finally succeeded in making this difficult recipe. I would like to hear you praise it."

"You won't believe it, but today I saw the Blessed Virgin in a dream, and she said to me, 'Give a plate of beans to the person you love best outside your own family; otherwise you'll get the measles for the second time.' Uncle, there's no one I love more than you, and I don't want the measles."

Uncle Salim ate to ward off the measles, to confirm a husband's opinion that his wife could cook like a dream, to determine whether perhaps a pinch of coriander—which could just as well have been left out—was missing, but every week he got a splendid meal.

May 28 — I always read Nadia's letters over and over again. In one of them she writes, "Even if they tear my heart out, I will love you with all that remains."

I told this to Mahmud, who was ashamed of having had such a bad opinion of her. We absolutely must devise a way that I can meet her without her parents catching on.

June 10 — For twelve days I haven't written a word!

I suspect, although I'm not entirely certain, that Mariam is having an affair with Habib. Today she was at his place. Habib was in a state; he was curt and did not want to let me in, but Mariam said, "He's a good boy!"

Somehow her remark is eating at me. I'm not a good boy! What does she mean by that? I have to know! Perhaps Habib is the cause of her sudden fits of cheerfulness. What a dope I am to think she loves me! A good boy? What does she know anyway?

June 14 — Mahmud has written his second play. The protagonist, of course, is Ahmad Malas. A gruesome story:

An editor at a radio station has become famous, but he no longer gets any ideas. A colleague gives him a tip. Go to the prison, he tells him; the inmates will gladly tell stories for a pack of cigarettes and sometimes even free of charge. Spiced up a bit, the stories could be quite torrid. And what a sensation it would be if one of the prisoners were to stand at a microphone and talk about all the murders, thefts, and frauds he had committed. Everybody listening would flip. If the editor could get hold of some photos of the prisoners, he could also publish the stories in a newspaper and kill two birds with one stone.

Mahmud describes the editor as someone who kills himself—but no birds—with two stones. The editor goes to the prison, but the inmates will not speak before a microphone for all the money in the world. They have suffered enough over the years and have had enough trouble already because of some statements they'd made. After much hemming and hawing, a few prisoners do agree to tell their life stories, provided that the editor only takes notes and does not name any names. He consents to this and collects a heap of material, most of it pretty boring. Nevertheless, spiced up and condensed into one character, the awful picture of a beast emerges.

A colleague gives the unimaginative editor a second

tip. There are many old actors with piles of debts and no jobs who could play the part of the criminal. After a long search, he finds an old actor who agrees to do it, providing that at the end of the series the editor comes clean about everything.

The series begins, and the beastly character describes with pleasure how he strangles grannies and grandpas, mugs passersby, steals food out of the mouths of babes and abuses them. He makes faces and lets himself be photographed with disheveled hair and a stubbly beard; the newspapers sell out.

Now comes the third episode, the last. On the radio and in the newspaper, the editor concludes it without keeping his word, without saying the man is an actor. The man's neighbors avoid him; many people spit at him. Even merchants won't sell him anything; his face is better known in the town than the president's. The poor devil goes back to the radio station again and again, but the editor will not see him. When, after hours of waiting, the actor finally manages to get in, the editor promises that tomorrow or the next day he will publish the truth. After a month, the man is a complete wreck. In the end, the tattered, starved actor lies in wait for the editor and slays him. The newspapers publish a fourth installment, the radio airs a fourth episode, and the neighbors breathe more easily now that the man is finally behind bars.

Mahmud forgets nothing. Whether a theater will ever perform this play is another matter. I have told Habib and Uncle Salim about it, and they are enthusiastic. I didn't much like the part about the neighbors, but Mahmud says that people will believe anything if they hear it often enough.

June 24 — We have all known sorrow. Last Wednesday, there was a lot going on in the bakery. No sooner had I finished my noon rounds and was about to rest than the axle of the dough machine broke. My father was actually quite calm and replaced it with one he had in reserve. He was just saying, "We have all earned a nice pot of tea," when a police car pulled up in front of the bakery. Two policemen hurried out, stationed themselves at the door, and barred it with their machine guns. A man in a fine suit slowly got out of the car and gazed at our bakery. Nervously my father dried his hands on the edge of his apron and whispered, "Blessed Mary, protect me! Blessed Mary, stand by me!"

The elegantly dressed man was about thirty. He asked for my father by name, and as my poor father answered him, without moving a muscle in his face the man said, "Come along!"

"What have I done, sir?"

"You needn't be afraid if you haven't done anything," the man answered very softly, and by gesturing—it was no more than a tiny wink of an eye—commanded the policemen to drive the grumbling customers away from the door. At once the two officers pushed people with the butts of their guns. My father looked on, horrified. I had never seen him so pale.

"Where to?" he asked helplessly. "I mean, should I remove my apron and take a jacket along?"

"Yes, that would be better; take your jacket along," the man said.

"Blessed Mary," my father whispered. He took his jacket from the hook, threw his apron in the corner, then stroked my hair. "Don't be afraid, my boy. I'll be right back," he murmured and went out.

When one of the policemen handcuffed my father, my paralysis left me. I rushed outside and grabbed my father's jacket, trying to pull him away as he was being thrust into the car. One of the policemen hit me, but I held on tight and cried for help. Then he struck me in the belly and I reeled backward. Two of the bakery workers caught me. One of them called out loud, "You filthy dogs. He is still just a child!"

The car sped away. The frightened neighbors hurried by, and the florist brought me a glass of water. "Drink this, my boy. It's good for shock. Only God remains on high. All assholes plummet down!"

That night we could not sleep. My mother wept, and the neighbors came in shifts and sat up with her. Uncle Salim didn't sleep either. At four in the morning, without saying a word, he accompanied me to the bakery. He took over the cash register, letting the employees advise him what to do. I made deliveries to my customers and shot back to the bakery like an arrow. I no longer felt the least bit tired. I didn't want to leave my old friend alone any more than necessary; he is over seventy-five and nearsighted. But all day long he made jokes and reassured the customers that my father would soon return.

For four days they worked my father over. Twice they toyed with a pistol at his temples, threatening to shoot if he did not tell the truth. When my father declared over and over that he didn't even know what they wanted from him, they pulled the trigger. The pistol was not loaded, but my father fainted. There's something he didn't do when they beat him up: He did not cry and did not beg for leniency. But he did see other prisoners break down.

"Say who you are," a policeman demanded of an old

farmer. The poor devil uttered his name, and the policeman beat him until he got the desired answer, "I am a
dog! I am a traitor!" And when another one called out
"For God's sake," his torturer laughed, took a second
cudgel, and said, "Take this, for God's sake." My father
wept like a child when he told us this. Uncle Salim
kissed his eyes and held his hand.

Four days the scoundrels beat my father, until they
discovered they had confused him with a lawyer who
had worked against the government and who happened
to have the same name.

Uncle Salim doesn't buy this story. "They hit you to
make our knees go weak. They know very well that your
father and your mother have different names and that
you are a baker," he said and cursed the government.

I had never been so proud of my father as I was today.
Since the beating, I love him as never before. It's good I
didn't run away. My parents could not have survived
that; the first thing my father would have done upon returning was ask for me.

I will never forgive the government. "Whoever forgives
injustice, gets more injustice," Uncle Salim said when I
confided to him my hatred.

Father has asked us not to tell anyone about the torture, because the pigs threatened to torment him for
months if he said a word about it to anyone. But I told
Mahmud, and he thinks as Uncle Salim does. A wave of
indiscriminate arrests is rolling over Damascus, bringing
many people grief and humiliation.

I almost forgot, but before I finish for today, I must
write something about this. When Uncle Salim turned
over the receipts from the four days, my father wanted
to pay him for his work, but the good man declined to

accept even a single piaster. Then I begged my father, for my sake, to invite him to dinner with us every Sunday.

Uncle Salim accepted this invitation with his usual wit. "I would love to, because then I can tell my friend some of my foolish stories; he'll forget about his food, and I'll get two portions."

June 26 — Nadia slipped me a letter. She wrote quite lovingly of how she had just heard about my father last night. Her father said that many suspects had been arrested and interrogated and that once again the government had averted a coup. She says she despises her father, a man who licks the ass of each successive government. Great!

June 29 — I wanted Habib to tell me about the wave of arrests that was going on, but I didn't want to tell him about my father. Since he lives a little ways from us, he hadn't witnessed it. I asked, and Habib only grew still; he did not answer. After a while he asked if I had read the Gibran. I shouted that Gibran was of no interest to me just now; I wanted to know about the arrests because a friend of mine had been detained for no reason. He kept silent and looked sorrowfully into my eyes.

"For no reason? Since when does this government need a reason to torture people?" He laughed like a madman, stood up, and banged his fist against the wall. I was scared, because the whole time he was staring at me with wide-open eyes. I would have liked to get out of there. But then he calmed down.

"Ask your father if he needs anyone in the bakery. I would so much like to work for him, to work for a loaf of bread," he said as we parted.

A strange fellow this Habib!

July 10 — Today I know that Mariam loves Habib! It was my own doing, but now I regret my eagerness. She loves him and not me. My doubts have plagued me these last few days. Though I love Nadia, I still wanted to know Mariam's feelings for me and for Habib. Yesterday I asked if she loved him. She said she didn't. She said she thought he was a very nice man but had no further interest in him whatsoever. (My God, how she stressed this!) She said she liked me but that I'm very young. She's right. But she still loves Habib.

Yesterday I told her how my father was tortured, and I asked her not to repeat this to anyone. She had not known what had happened, though she had wondered why for four days I hadn't had any time for her. Habib hadn't even noticed!

July 11 — Today I brought Habib his bread and wanted to get on with my rounds, but he insisted I spend some time with him. He was drunk again, as he so often has been lately. I did not want to disappoint him and so I went in. He made me some tea and suddenly asked why I had not told him my father had been arrested and tortured. Just now I don't know how I came up with the reply, "Because you work for the official government newspaper."

Never in my life will I forget how he looked at me! Not only was he filled with surprise, sorrow, and rage, but a kind of shame was mixed in. I looked away because I knew my answer had hurt him deeply. Softly he murmured that he would not be able to work for the paper much longer. It would be the death of him. Many of his friends had been arrested, and he wasn't permitted to write about it. He spoke of his loneliness; his voice became sadder and sadder, but he did not cry. Without shedding a tear, he described how the previous regime had tortured him and shot his wife, how he had fled the country and returned only when his party had come into power. In the interim his friend had become editor in chief, and an important editorial post had been arranged for Habib. But in less than a year he had a falling out with his friend, who had turned the newspaper—just as the previous governments had—into a scandal sheet. And Habib relinquished his dreams of a lovely house and a company car. Many journalists have fled, but Habib is already fifty years old; he's tired of running and just wants to go on living.

All at once I felt compassion for him. Within half an hour all the fear I'd had of him in the previous months was gone; I lit a cigarette. Habib didn't even notice.

"What will you do?" he asked as I left.

"You will soon see," I answered tersely.

July 22 — I spoke to Mahmud, and we've decided on a course of action against three spies who live in our neighborhood. Nadia's father resides on our street; the second man lives on the same street as the school; the third one, near Habib's apartment.

Mahmud didn't want to say anything to Josef, since Josef is becoming more and more zealous about the army. We drafted a brief message and signed it in the name of the Black Hand: *Don't forget this, you spies! We are like camels. We forget nothing, and one day you will be punished.*

July 29 — The fox is said to be the cleverest animal on earth. But I think man is foxier than the sliest fox. Mahmud demonstrated this today.

Mahmud's father always buys two kinds of tea: one that is cheap, for the family, since his nine children drink huge quantities every day, and a fine Ceylon blend for himself. He keeps the latter under lock and key.

Today Mahmud's mother took eight of her children to visit a friend; Mahmud stayed home. His father returned from work, washed himself, and made his tea. Suddenly he discovered there was no sugar in the house. As he feared for his precious tea, he put it in the cupboard with wire-mesh doors, locked the doors, and hurried to the shop around the corner to buy some sugar.

Mahmud observed him all the while from my window, and when his father was out of the house, Mahmud crept into the kitchen. Adroitly he stuck a straw through the mesh, pushed the teapot lid aside, and slurped and savored the tea. Because the tea was still very hot, he blew between gulps, but this did not prevent Mahmud from emptying the pot. With the straw still in hand, he rushed over to my room. We waited until his father came back wheezing.

Never in my life will I forget his father's face when he took the pot out of the closet and looked into its empty belly. First he pronounced two well-known charms from the Koran against evil spirits, but then he paused and cried out: "Mahmuuuuuud! Come here at once!" When Mahmud appeared at the door, looking innocent as a lamb, his father stared at him and laughed, "Have you burned your mouth at least?" Mahmud nodded mischievously.

August 3 — Josef was insanely angry. He learned of our action from Nadia's brother. He's afraid his dream of becoming an officer will be ended if this comes out.

There was much yelling, and he said we had no right to misuse the name of the gang he had founded. If we do it again, he will turn us in!

August 7 — Met Josef on the street, and he greeted me very coolly and hurried away. He didn't want to be seen with me anymore. Funny!

August 14 — Uncle Salim told me a story he had heard. He did not name the country, but I believe these events could occur at many borders nowadays:

A traveler was laughing at his fellow passengers as they approached the border. The man was strangely dressed; all he wore was a towel tied around his bottom.

"You have chocolate, you a radio, and you a cassette recorder," he said, laughing. "They will be taken from you at the border. I know this country; you can't bring anything into it."

The man was unpleasant to the other people and did not tire of badgering them. "What do you have there? A watch, a shirt. And you there, how do you expect to get through with that coat?"

The closer they came to the border, the more and more nervous the people became. Slowly they grasped why this fellow was practically naked; even the towel he wore was made in that country.

When the coach reached the border, the customs officials were even more severe with each passenger than the near-naked traveler had predicted. He remained seated, chuckling while the customs officers confiscated everything: radios, chocolate, and coat.

When it was his turn, he exulted. "I am naked, and the towel has been manufactured in your country!"

"You know a lot, don't you?" the customs officer asked, completely deadpan.

"Yes, I read a lot!" the man gloated.

"And what do you read?" the officer inquired.

The man enumerated many books, and the official patiently made a note of each title and politely asked whether he was spelling the names of the authors correctly.

No sooner had the man stopped than the customs official asked, "Is that all?" And the man boasted of a whole new series of books he had read. The official wrote everything down, until the man realized he was being tricked. He fell silent.

"So," the official said to the know-it-all, "you're carrying two hundred books in your head and want to sneak them in. And half of these books are forbidden. Oh, these smugglers, always coming up with new methods!" he grumbled, and sent the naked man back where he had come from.

August 16 — At the Abassie Theater, pornographic films are shown once a month, at a secret noon screening. The wily theater owner bribes the police, who close their eyes and ears. The tickets don't cost the usual one pound; they cost three. The swine makes a fortune through these monthly showings.

The theater is new and gigantic, and the several hundred spectators learn by word of mouth which day the skin-flick will be shown. The day is supposedly kept a secret so the police won't find out. But how, Mahmud asks me, does it happen the police don't know when over six hundred people show up for movies in the midday heat? These same police officers know at once when five people meet for tea and warn them they've been under surveillance for weeks.

Today I went there with Mahmud for the first time. The troop of people streaming in looked like a protest march. There was no one at the box office and no advance notice, but each person just happened to have a ticket somehow or other.

It was a titillating film, showing nothing but European strip-tease joints. When the lights came on, I looked right into the eyes of my former math teacher. He turned red, and I felt my own ears get hot. He didn't say hello, nor did I. Each of us gazed off in a different direction. Mahmud didn't realize what was going on. When I told him once we got outside, he laughed at my inhibitions.

August 20 — "Ah! I've been waiting for you!" Habib greeted me today when I came with his bread. I wanted to leave, but he insisted that I have breakfast with him. I still had half an hour before my noon rounds, so I stayed.

"You did that well," he said, grinning.

"What have I done well?" I asked, somewhat confused.

"The business with the Black Hand, you rogue!"

I must have seemed paralyzed, for he laughed and said, "Swallow that piece of bread so you don't choke on it!" He pressed my arm. "You needn't be afraid. I alone know. The idiots at the newspaper learned about it from the secret service. Of course we're not allowed to write a word about it, but when I heard the name of our street, I was sure. The chief really believes it's a gang, and is already scared shitless. Congratulations!"

"But you haven't told Mariam anything," I said, once I had caught my breath.

"Why do you ask about Mariam?" Habib asked, astonished.

"I know—but that dope of a husband of hers doesn't," I replied. We laughed like two conspirators. For the first time I felt a certain closeness to Habib. How long it sometimes takes to penetrate to the core of another human being!

"Do you really want to be a journalist? Actually, you already are one, but if you'd like to learn a few trifles, then . . ."

"Yes!" I interrupted him, enthusiastic. "Please teach me!"

"Starting today, come every evening at six for an hour. I'd be very pleased to show you some things, Colleague!" he said. For the first time he embraced me as I left.

August 26 — "Today the six months are up!" Uncle Salim said. "Do you regret your decision?"

I had long since forgotten our agreement, but this friend never just talks off the top of his head. His promise is sacred to him.

"No, I'm glad I stayed," I answered. In fact, I don't regret it. Here I will become a journalist!

August 29 — Mr. Katib stopped by my father's bakery today and gave him two copies of the book in which my poems appear. By the time I got there, he was already gone. My father beamed at me.

"There's my young poet!" he cried. Two customers, an old woman and the tiler from next door, did not understand who he meant by poet or why my old man was so cheerful. He quickly pressed their loaves of bread into their hands and embraced me. Then he had two cups of tea brought to us.

"How much will you pay for some good news?" he asked, keeping me on tenterhooks.

"The poems . . . have . . . come out!" I exclaimed.

"What a miser!" my father replied, enjoying himself. "And I wanted to be the one to tell you! All right, here they are." He took two copies out of the closet. My heart was beating so hard I could scarcely breathe. Weak-kneed, I sat down on a stool and looked at the books.

The cover bore the title *The Flying Tree: Poems by Young People.* I could not believe my eyes. The publisher had named the entire volume after my poem! The book is so incredibly beautiful! The title page is a watercolor in which a blue moon gazes toward a flying tree, whose leaves look like swallows and stars. My hand glided over the pages, and I searched for my name both in the table of contents and inside the book.

In his foreword the publisher tells about my meeting with him. He writes of having had financial difficulties with the book, but after talking to me—he even mentions my name—he was convinced that the book should be done, cost what it may. What a day! I took the book with me on my noon rounds. After every two customers, I sat down somewhere and read and read; I couldn't get enough. The poems of the other young people are also great!

Habib wasn't home. Mariam wanted the book, but I told her she would have to buy her own copy because one of my copies was for Habib and the other for myself, my parents, and Mahmud.

I practically flew home, and when I reached Nadia's door, I knocked, without even thinking of the danger or her brothers. Her mother came out smiling and looked at me in astonishment.

"My poems have appeared. I want to show them to Nadia!"

Nadia immediately came running. "We're in luck; those two aren't here!" she said breathlessly. "Beautiful! How very beautiful!" she whispered and, with the most loving hand on earth, stroked the moon in the book and then my face. I pushed her into the dark corridor and kissed her lips.

"So that's why you wanted to write poems," she teased me, laughing.

I ran home like a maniac. My mother thought I had gone nuts. I sang louder than ever—I know I sing like a rusty watering can; that's why I normally spare myself and others—but today I sang wildly and in languages I don't know, and my mother laughed and asked if a snake had bitten me. I told her I had to vent these shrieks because I'd been carrying them around inside me not just all day but for months. Exultant, I grabbed her by her waist and whirled her around.

Once I had calmed down a bit, I told her, "Mr. Katib said he would read my poems aloud in class so the other students will think of me. And he'll do this every year, so they won't forget me!"

My mother began to bawl. "Mr. Katib is such a splendid person. We are very poor, but the Blessed Virgin Mary will hear me and guard your life. She always hears the prayers of mothers."

I begged her to stop going on about the Virgin Mary. We ought to be celebrating, not crying. I went and got twenty pounds and gave them to her. She was to buy two kilos of coffee and one kilo of tea.

"And what about me?" Leila piped up, as if the neighbors alone were going to drink the tea. Fine, I gave her a pound, and in the course of the late afternoon she bought a sundae, nuts, chewing gum, and cotton candy; afterward she felt sick to her stomach. My mother made her some strong anise tea. Leila suspected that things had gone so badly because I did not give her the pound with my whole heart. Can she ever tell tales!

P.S.: At six o'clock I went to Habib's. He wasn't half surprised about the book I gave him. "You really are a character," he said and for an hour explained how a newspaper article is put together.

Sunday — Uncle Salim had dinner with us today. It was delightful. My father praised the good tea I had provided.

September 1 — My parents are showing the book to everyone. Habib tirelessly instructs me about newspaper work and shows me how to write an engrossing article. He himself, however, is desperately unhappy about his work. He will help me get out of the bakery. A friend of his has a bookstore in the New City. My father is doing well; we no longer have any debts. The bakery brings in enough to live on.

September 3 — Mahmud told me about yesterday's boxing match. Syria's most famous boxer is a third-rate thug who got nowhere abroad. Again and again he beats up frail Syrian opponents, who must then venerate him as undefeated.

For weeks posters were plastered on every wall in Damascus. The boxer had challenged a United States champion; Mr. Black Fire accepted the challenge and came to Damascus. Tickets sold for over twenty pounds on the black market. Many people just wanted to see the bitter defeat of the Syrian braggart; they were siding with the black guest, especially since he had some good words for Arabs and Syrians. He was interviewed by newspapers, magazines, and the radio in his expensive hotel, the Samir Amis. Others, especially the supporters of the Syrian show-off, wanted a definitive confirmation that there was something more than fat beneath the skin of their colossus. The whole town spoke of nothing but this fight. I don't generally like boxing, but one of the journalists in the café got Mahmud a ticket.

The boxer from America really must have looked terrifying. He stomped around the ring, bellowing in English, repeatedly wanting to attack the spectators in the first few rows who were making fun of him. Then the fight began. The first round drew to a leisurely conclusion. The second fell more to the guest than to the boaster. The spectators spurred the staggering, shattered Syrian fighter on. In the third round, he fought his opponent hard and mercilessly knocked him down. With his last ounce of strength, the American dragged himself into his corner, and the spectators—opponents and supporters both—cheered the Syrian colossus, inciting him to punch wildly in the fourth round. Suddenly he hit the guest forcefully on the nose, causing him to reel backward and begin to scream—in Arabic!

Mr. Black Fire ran in front of the colossus and wailed into the hall that he was not American but Palestinian. "Help, help, he wants to kill me!" he screeched loudly, staggering around the ring on unsteady feet and trying to hide behind the referee. "This was not the agreement!"

he cried over and over, letting the referee take the punches. Now the Syrian colossus wanted to silence him with a K.O., but time and again he hit the referee. The crowd began to rampage, demolishing the seats and, after a drawn-out fight with the police, left the hall.

"He was a Palestinian," the journalists reported, "who for a little money and a few nights of luxury in a hotel participated in this rotten game. The Syrian boxer had promised to hit him gently; only in the fifteenth round was he to fall on cue and simulate a K.O."

When I told Uncle Salim about it, he laughed for a long time. "You see, my boy, this boxing match is just like Arabian politics."

September 5 — Habib is pressing me to say something to my father once and for all. His friend has agreed to hire me, being in need of someone who loves books. Uncle Salim says it's now or never. I have to do it alone, and without too much deliberation. Sometimes I think too much. Tomorrow I'll take the plunge.

September 6 — Fabulous! When I told my old man that I wanted to leave the bakery in order to work for a bookdealer, all he did was nod.

"Selling books is an honorable profession!" He was quiet a while. "A bookdealer," he repeated, "that's good. You were not born for the bakery. I've always known that. You love books, so go ahead!"

Habib, my mother, and above all Uncle Salim congratulated me. Now I'm looking for a baker's apprentice I can train in one week, and then I'm out of here. Only Mariam was unhappy. I calmed her, saying I would be at her friend Habib's every day. She did not even react to my using the word *friend*!

September 11 — For three days now I have been going around with the apprentice. A clever young man from a village on the Lebanese border. He is full of plans; he wants to be an actor. He has a beautiful voice, and when he sings in the bakery, even my father listens.

Not only does he have a lovely voice, he can also imitate famous actors incredibly well; best of all is his imitation of Charlie Chaplin. Many passersby grimace and say, "You'll go crazy fooling around like that." If he has a friend as good as Uncle Salim, he will become an actor.

September 15 — Today was my first day in the bookstore. Though it's not very big, five of us work there. All I got to do was the dirty work: fetch cartons of books from the storeroom, open them, repack them, dust the shelves, clean the big window, make tea, and be available. I have neither sold books nor wrapped them for the customers. The others do these things.

My boss said I ought to learn everything from the bottom up; otherwise I'll never be a good bookdealer. He's an odd bird. He claims that when he started out, he had to put his master's house and garden in order. Clearly he's stretching the truth. But he calls Habib his best friend.

I'm earning only half of what I was in the bakery, but I'm not half so tired as I was there. At noon we have more than an hour off, and today during that time I read a short story—sad and beautiful—by a Russian author.

September 18 — Mahmud had a rotten day. A customer had it in for him. At first the man was friendly and invited Mahmud to have a lemonade. Mahmud, however, declined. Somehow or other the man was unappealing.

Suddenly the coffee was no good; Mahmud brought him another cup. No, now he wanted tea. Mahmud gave the coffee to another customer and brought some tea. The man became insolent and screamed at Mahmud for having touched the rim of the cup; he would not drink from it. Mahmud brought him a new cup. The man had his tea and went over to the counter, where he complained that Mahmud had said, "Here, now gulp down your shitty tea!" Mahmud had said no such thing, but his boss believed the guest and pulled Mahmud by the ear. Then Mahmud got furious and punched the loudly laughing guest in the stomach. He was fired!

He doesn't dare tell his father about it, and he badly needs a new job.

September 25 — A whole week has gone by, and although Mahmud has been searching from morning until night, he can't find a job. I had to advance him three pounds today so he could give them to his father. He said he would never forget this. I believe him; he's a good friend. Until he finds a position, I will give him three pounds a week from my reserves. After all, I have saved nearly two hundred and fifty pounds.

October 2 — Now another week has passed, and Mahmud is still out of work. Searching for work is so humiliating, and he hates the customer who destroyed everything for him. Like a beggar, he goes from shop to shop. Perhaps today he'll have luck with a Jewish tailor at the bazaar. I have also asked the bookdealer, but he doesn't need anyone.

Every day I learn more and more during my hour at Habib's. A journalist's job is extremely complicated.

Nadia's eldest brother is volunteering for the army. The army's a good place for that idiot. In a week we'll be rid of him; he's going up north to start a course in radar. Her other brother is staying in school; he's not as bad as the older one.

October 9 — Nadia's eldest brother is finally in Aleppo. To celebrate this day, Nadia and I met for an hour. With her mother's knowledge. She asked us to be careful and cautioned Nadia to come back on time (her other brother comes home from school at four; her father returns at five). It was wonderful to feel her small fingers in my hand again.

As an exercise I was supposed to write about a book-dealer's profession; I was also supposed to interview my boss. And I did. But words spilled from him as from a waterfall, so I couldn't get very much down. Then I sat working on the article for several days.

Habib read it, thrust it aside, and screamed: "Catastrophe! C-a-t-a-s-t-r-o-p-h-e-e-e-e-e-e!!! Idiot that I am, what have I taught you? Eh? What is this? You just gloss over things, and it's boring, too!" He pulled himself together and proceeded to point out the parts of the article I had simply made up.

October 10 — Mahmud has a new job! He says his boss is a nice old man; the pay isn't bad, and his father doesn't mind that he's changed jobs. He wanted to pay back the six pounds little by little, but I made them a gift. This did my dear friend Mahmud good.

Nadia's parents went out visiting, so I sneaked over to see her. Today, for the first time, I kissed her properly—neck, breasts, and belly. She has such beautiful skin! She sighed with contentment, then said, with reproach in her voice, "You seem to have a lot of experience!"

I boasted that I knew still more and that when her parents were gone for a longer time, I would prove it to her. Bragging like that made me feel powerful, but what if Nadia really believes me?

October 11 — Day and night the radio blares that people should work harder. Uncle Salim said he no longer understands the world. "These imbeciles!" he groaned over and over as we sat drinking tea and listening. Then a singer praised working in the fields and in factories, saying he longed to get his hands on a sickle and to hear the beating of a hammer on an anvil. Uncle Salim turned off the radio in disgust. "What a blathering idiot! Clearly he's never had a sickle in his hand. Gripping it burns your skin, and that's what this nincompoop longs for. Let him work in the fields in June sometime; then he'll sing a different tune—'How lovely is the shade!' "

October 12 — A happy coincidence: Uncle Salim wanted to go to the barber and so did I. We ambled along the street to the Thomas Gate. The old Armenian was in a particularly bad mood today, but we had a good laugh nonetheless.

"Do you know Michail?" the barber's assistant asked Uncle Salim as he walked into the shop.

Just about everyone knows Michail the Colossus, a butcher who breeds pigeons on his roof. Breeders of pigeons are usually at war with one another and with their neighbors: with one another out of envy; with their neighbors because the breeders often throw pebbles and orange peels at the birds, which land on their neighbors' heads and in their food. The pigeons also frequently shit on their terraces and leave tracks on the laundry and on fruits and vegetables spread out to dry.

"One evening," the assistant said, "Michail was sitting down to a meal with his wife when suddenly he heard steps on the roof. He grabbed hold of his stick and crept upstairs. A rival was attempting to steal his best pigeon. The fowl, a rare beauty, was said to be worth a hundred pounds. Just as the thief was about to open the cage, Michail grabbed him by the neck, threw him to the ground, and beat him with his stick, all the while shrieking to his wife to go get the police. Which she did. In the meantime, Michail carried the frail, unconscious thief outside and waited for the cops to arrive. With the stick in his left mitt and the poor devil under his arm, he cried out: 'Where is the state that protects its citizens?'

"The neighbors sat down with him, looking forward to an enjoyable scene. After a while an old policeman came along on a bicycle. He fought his way through the crowd and asked what was wrong. The thief was practically himself again, but he waited for the policeman to come closer. Only then did he tear himself free from the butcher's powerful grip and fall at the feet of the man of law and order, imploring him, 'Help me, please! This man wants to kill me!'

" 'Throw him in jail,' Michail demanded in a rage.

"The policeman looked at the anxious thief, whose head and face were completely swollen, and said, 'He should be in a hospital, not in prison. Better bring him a lemonade, some bandages, and iodine. Otherwise he'll die, and I'll have to arrest you for grave bodily harm!'

" 'Lemonade! Why not some *arrack* too?' Michail bellowed. Nothing made any sense; he raised his arm and clobbered the policeman over the head. The man fell to the ground unconscious."

Uncle Salim guffawed, but when the master barber grumbled something in Armenian, the assistant fell silent and quickly finished cutting Uncle Salim's hair. But he kept laughing and winking at Uncle Salim.

October 13 — Lately I've been reading a lot and discussing what I read with Habib. My boss has nothing against my reading or even taking a book home with me, provided I don't fold the corners of the pages or bring the book back soiled.

Habib read the second draft of my article about the bookdealer. All he said, drily, was "It's okay." I need to bring more life into it, so that people who are not bookdealers can really understand it, too.

October 15 — In Damascus it is often not easy to distinguish between legend and truth. Not far from here an innocuous man by the name of Saul was converted to Christianity by a vision and became Paul, a prince of the Church. Uncle Salim says that "the Damascus experience" is one of the city's specialties. Damascene steel and silk are famous, but I've never heard of this specialty before. Uncle Salim also says that time and again Damascus imports a Saul, processes him into a Paul, and then unleashes him upon humanity.

Saul was a persecutor of Christians. One day he came to Damascus from Jerusalem in order to track down the followers of Christ, seize them, and take them back with him to Jerusalem. Just outside Damascus, it is said, Jesus appeared to him as a bright light and rebuked Saul for persecuting him. Saul fell to the ground; when he stood up, he was blind. A man by the name of Ananias healed his eyes and converted him to Christianity. Ananias Lane is a couple of hundred meters away from my street. A small church, also bearing the name of Ananias, is situated there.

Paul, too, was persecuted, once he became a Christian, and he was also considered a traitor. For a long time he hid from the soldiers who pursued him. What would have happened on this earth if Paul—who one night sneaked down my street and who, in the end, was forced to escape by being lowered over the city wall in a basket—had been caught and killed? Without Paul there would be no Christianity today. He built up the entire apparatus of the Church. Am I going on about this too much? Still, it seems that my street, with its clay houses, was responsible for a major world development—all because Paul escaped down it. It is even said that he had to wait in the last hut against the wall for two whole days until the coast was clear. Is this a fairy tale?

The madman is right when he says that life is a rainbow with all its colors. Some people see only one striking color and cry aloud, "How lovely this green rainbow is!" But the rainbow would be tiresome if it were only green. The other colors, delicately remaining in the background, are what make up the rainbow. My street is one of those hidden colors.

Habib told me about the tenth-century state, the Republic of the Qarmatians. No sultan, no rich, and thus no poor existed in this republic. All anybody owned was his clothing and his sword. Women, too, had their say and were allowed to divorce their husbands. There were kindergartens for children. The arduous work of milling grain, which prior to the time of the republic was accomplished solely by the women and which completely wore them out, was taken over by the central mill.

A council of six headed the state and could at any time be removed from office by the state assembly. The members of the council were unpaid and had to earn their living by other means. Children grew up without religion and without bans. The republic explained that all people were equal. It abolished the slavery that had previously been accepted as God-given. It explained the meaning of peace to all peoples.

The republic survived for one hundred and fifty years. First it extended from the region of the Persian Gulf all the way to Iraq and Syria, but then its arch-enemies, the rulers of the surrounding nations, banded together, and the much-hated republic fell under their swords. The enemies of the Qarmatian Republic let no child or woman escape. They were considered to be contaminated—of course with the most dangerous bacillus of all time, freedom.

When Habib begins to talk about the Qarmatian Republic, he simply does not stop. His eyes take on a strange glow. But he doesn't believe a word of the legend of Paul; he says it's a dull tale, invented in retrospect, so that Christians would have tangible places and persons. He may not believe it, but our school books are absolutely silent about the Qarmatians and their republic. An epoch of one hundred and fifty years doesn't rate a single line in our history books! Nonetheless, we are very well informed about what the caliph Hārūn ar-Rashīd did when he once couldn't sleep, and exactly what the other caliphs said and how they expressed themselves in various circumstances, and when they were bumped off, and how long they ruled.

My mother believes every letter of the story of Paul, but when I told her about the Qarmatian women, she said Habib must have heard this story from his mother. Because she knows that all women in the world tell stories like these, not because they have happened, but because they ought to happen.

How much of this is true or false does not interest me. These stories persist, and we live in their midst.

October 20 — For days one question has preoccupied me. How does one write an article about beggars? I suggested this theme as an exercise, and Habib agreed to it.

The new mayor of Damascus sends his police force out to hunt beggars. When he took office, he promised to rid Damascus of them within half a year. Beggars allegedly make the city look bad to tourists. I spoke to some beggars and to Uncle Salim and came up with three pages; Habib doesn't like long articles.

I wrote that I found the new mayor genuinely stupid for persecuting the poor and not poverty. If tourists stay away because of them, then a monument to beggars ought to be erected (old Salim gave me this idea). The mayor comes from one of the wealthiest families in the north. His grandparents owned whole villages, including the inhabitants. His father has a bank, and now the son wants to persecute the very people his parents and grandparents put out of work. For many beggars were once craftsmen or farmers who lost everything and came to Damascus in the hope of finding work. The beggars, I wrote, understand more about people and their souls than many schoolteachers. All they need do is look at someone, and instantly they know how to address that person. Does the mayor know how to do this?

October 29 — Today, when I got to Habib's place, he was rather down. I sat for one whole hour. He didn't say a word; he just smoked and slowly, very slowly, drank a glass of *arrack*. At some point I'd had enough and wanted to leave, but all of a sudden he asked if I had written my piece on the beggars of Damascus.

I gave him the article, and he began to read it. From one page to the next his eyes became happier, and at the end he laughed out loud and slapped his thigh.

"My dear boy! This is good! This hits home!" He gave me his hand. "Now you are a colleague! I can't teach you anything more. Let's have a toast."

He poured me a small glass of *arrack*. I don't like the stuff. It has a very strong taste, rather like soap. I took a gulp and started to cough. Habib laughed. "And don't forget every author's golden rule: Write every day, even if it is only half a page."

I will never forget this!

P.S.: Habib said the article was so good that the state newspaper would never publish it. That was supposed to be praise. What a stupid paper!

November 3 — A customer came into the shop, asking for advice. He wanted to buy two books for his son: a volume of poems (naturally I recommended the best— ours) and a novel, Maxim Gorki's *Mother*. But first he wanted to know more about the Russian author's book. Not long ago, I had read it over the course of three nights. I thoroughly identified with the hero. It was the best book I'd ever read, and I managed to convince the man of this. My boss was delighted and rubbed his palms.

November 11 — In our bookshop alone one hundred copies of the poetry anthology have been sold. The publisher wrote us an enthusiastic letter, thanking us for our investment and informing us that the book had been well received everywhere. Now my boss is putting *The Flying Tree* in the window.

November 12 — Habib is different from Uncle Salim. However much he may like me, he never tells me about himself. I find out things about him from Mariam, or not at all. He has been very sad lately and has been drinking and smoking a lot.

A general, alleged to be dangerous, was given a heap of money (all of it in gold and foreign currency) and fled to Latin America, where he purchased a huge farm and now lives like a lord. The government was said to have greased his palm with millions to get him out of the way. Habib wanted to write about it, but his boss, the editor in chief, gave him a talking-to about the article. He cannot possibly publish it. What really bothers Habib is that once, when they had fled abroad, he shared every bit of his bread with this editor in chief. At that time both of them had sworn to write only the truth.

November 16 — Today, through a friend, Habib got a French novel to translate. The author's name is Balzac. When I went to Habib's, things were going somewhat better for him; he had already begun the translation. He likes this Balzac a great deal and calls him the best French author of the nineteenth century. Suddenly he laughed demoniacally and said, "Balzac will be my springboard!"

I don't understand what he means. Does he want to leave the paper?

November 18 — Nadia has been taken out of school. Her father only meant to let her go through the first level of public examinations. She would very much like to become a pediatrician, but her father wants her to be a secretary for a famous lawyer.

November 19 — The madman with the sparrow has disappeared. The barber's assistant told us that the madman was suspected of being a spy. The sparrow was no ordinary bird; it was supposed to have a tiny camera, with which it flew around photographing secrets.

November 21 — Habib was not in. He seems to have forgotten our date. I didn't dare inquire at Mariam's; it was past six, and surely her husband was at home.

November 24 — For two days I have not been able to think of anything but Habib. He's been arrested! It's the talk of the town. He wrote an article concerning the plight of journalists who must lie to avoid attracting the attention of the government. By showing the censor a harmless article and getting authorization to publish it, Habib took the censor for a ride. With the official stamp on the article, Habib got it past the typesetters and printers. A few hours later the paper was sold out—perhaps for the first time!—and the entire editorial staff, including the editor in chief, was arrested.

My boss was upset and cursed the government because it did not even acknowledge the arrests in the following issue of the paper. The paper continues to appear as if nothing had happened; only those who read the fine print on the masthead can discern that the editorial staff is completely new.

I asked my boss for the afternoon off and hurried to see Mariam. To my great surprise, she knew all about it beforehand! Habib had told her the evening before his arrest. He had left an attaché case and the key to his apartment with her. She was supposed to give me the key, but no one was allowed to see the case.

Mariam wept for a long time and said that without Habib she could not go on. She must feel relieved though that her husband is doing well and is very sweet to her.

I took the key and hurried to Habib's apartment. What a strange feeling; it was so sad without him. For some reason or other, I began to tidy up the place. After a while Mariam joined me. When she went home toward six o'clock, I wanted to straighten up his clothes closet, and there I saw a picture of his wife. He had pasted it up inside the door and written with a felt-tip pen: "As long as I live I will avenge you."

I can't read or write except in my journal. Habib really is a brave man.

Thursday — Six days have gone by now, and Habib is still in prison. Uncle Salim is furious with the government. He, too, learned of the arrest without my telling him; every afternoon he listens to Radio London and Radio Israel. They mentioned Habib and read his article aloud. I haven't said a word about it to my father, but it's impossible to hide anything from my mother. First she asked about Nadia, and when she learned that things were all right between us, she said, "Then something must have happened to Habib; am I right?" I had to tell her.

December 1 — Nadia has been working in the law office for a week. She's bored and has to do everything—make coffee, distribute memos, deliver the mail, and sometimes even clean the desks. Next week she'll start a typing course. That's the only way she can better her position there; she has no desire to make coffee for the rest of her life.

The attorney she works for is very famous and employs five young lawyers. He treats them all rather badly. Nor does he have any respect for judges. He says they were all his students at the university, and were it not for him, they wouldn't be where they are.

Since Nadia started work, we always meet during lunch break. Her office is only three blocks away from the bookstore. I wait downstairs for her because her boss doesn't like it when one of his four secretaries goes out to meet a friend.

December 3 — Shopping with my mother is an experience! The bazaar is rather far away, and I rarely go there with her because it always takes so long. But today I accompanied her.

I am constantly amazed at how the merchants can recognize my mother among the thousands of customers who come to the bazaar month after month. They ask about my father, and she inquires about their wives and children. Sometimes she'll sit down at a booth, let the merchant show her fabric and clothing, have coffee, chat about herself, and listen to the merchant's chatter. Then she'll get up and go without buying anything, and the merchant isn't the least bit annoyed. But once she begins to bargain, I need the patience of Job. That's exactly what happened today.

My mother found some good material and asked how much it cost. The dealer named a price and stressed it was so low only because my pretty mother was a regular customer. Instead of rejoicing, she became angry and offered to pay half the sum. The merchant snatched it away and complained he wasn't such a fool as to sell his best fabric at a loss. He showed her some cloth of lesser quality at the price she named. My mother tested it, quickly running her hand over it, saying it wasn't all that bad, but she wanted the better cloth, for which she offered the merchant a few piasters more.

The merchant screamed in a rage and reproached my mother for being merciless toward his children but brought the price down a peg. The reproach of mercilessness should have moved my sensitive mother to tears, but she laughed, wished the children good health and happiness, and offered a few piasters more.

This time the man had a mild and funny reaction. He reminded my mother of the first time she had bought something from him. It was thirty years ago, but he still remembered her wearing a blue dress at the time and how pretty she looked. (She still looks marvelously pretty!) He further reminded her that the clothes she made from his fabric lasted for years, and then he lowered the price a little.

Instead of growing teary-eyed from so much praise, my mother reacted drily. Back then he had been very kind because he had been poor. But today he was rich and obstinate with a customer who passed up all the other merchants and came only to him. (This was not true. She had already checked out and priced the same material at other booths!) Nonetheless, she offered a few more piasters.

"What? So little?" the merchant moaned, indignant. "If my wife hears that I have sold this material so cheaply, she'll divorce me!"

"That wouldn't be a bad idea," my mother laughed. "Maybe she'll find a younger, better-looking merchant. You've grown too old and stingy," she added, offering a few more piasters.

The merchant laughed, praised my father for having married such a good, thrifty woman, and lowered his price somewhat but swore upon his pilgrimage to Mecca that this was his final offer.

My mother pretended she didn't know he had ever been to Mecca. "What? You, a pilgrim? I didn't know that. When did you go?"

The merchant described his laborious journey to Saudi Arabia and the sublime moment when he reached the holy place along with countless other believers. He didn't go into too much detail, knowing we are Christians, adding that at the next opportunity he would make a pilgrimage to Jerusalem. For Muslims, this is the second holy city after Mecca.

My mother got up and said on her way out, "You don't really want to sell it. I would have bought a great deal," and she offered him a new price, a few piasters higher than the last. Despairing—or at least seeming to despair—and with a loud groan, he gave my mother the cloth, forgot his oath, and did not neglect to ask her not to tell anyone she had bought the cloth so cheaply. He didn't want to be ruined.

Extremely happy at this turn of events, I took the bolt of fabric and hurried home with my mother. She praised the merchant and his honesty. I just don't get it.

December 6 — I had a marvelous time with Nadia. For the very first time I got to spend two whole hours alone with her. Her mother told me to look after her and send her home before five o'clock. (Even now I don't understand what she means by "look after." Was I supposed to protect Nadia from myself?) I went out alone, she followed, and we sneaked over to Habib's apartment. It was incredibly wonderful to lie beside her and caress her. She kissed me hard. The time went by so quickly; suddenly it was a quarter to five. Nadia hurried home, and I walked slowly at some distance behind her.

P.S.: Nadia thinks I must kiss so well either because I know a married woman or else because I have seen a lot of erotic films. I swore that I love no one but her. And films? Maybe I have seen a few skin-flicks but none in which the protagonist kisses the belly and legs of his beloved, which is exactly what Nadia likes best. We agreed to meet every Friday, my day off, at Habib's, even once Habib is out of jail. I will tell him this, and I'm sure he'll understand. After all, he loves Mariam!

Tuesday — What a delightful surprise: After three weeks, Habib was released today! Early in the morning he came to the bookstore. We gave him a frenzied welcome, and my boss had lemonade and coffee brought out. But Habib seemed bitter. When he asked me for his key, my boss told me to go with him. He furtively slipped twenty pounds into my pocket and whispered, "Get him something!"

Habib has a stubbly gray beard. It suits him and makes him look older. As I opened the door to his apartment, Mariam was already running up the stairs. She'd heard our voices in the stairwell. Habib embraced her and she kissed him.

When he saw the apartment, he was amazed at how neat and clean it was. "I think I should go to jail once a week," he said, smiling.

I disappeared for two hours and went shopping. I'm

no ogre! When I returned with a full shopping bag, Mariam was already gone. The bed looked as rumpled as ever. Habib had a loving smile on his face and was happy about the things I'd brought. He talked to me about prison for a long time.

Right now I'm dog tired; tomorrow I'll write it all down.

Wednesday — What Habib had to endure those three weeks sounds like an incredibly gruesome tale. With about fifteen other men, he was locked in a cell that had room for five at most. Ten of the prisoners had to stand close together so that five at a time could take turns lying down for a few hours. It wasn't always easy to maintain harmony among the prisoners; exhaustion made them aggressive, but after a while they were able to manage.

Habib had a very hard time. After all, he's a member of the ruling party. In the beginning the other prisoners wouldn't speak to him. At first they thought he was an informer and reproached him with all his party's atrocities. This hurt Habib more than the ruthless torture that was to come.

The next three days he was left in peace and could prepare himself for the trial. This, however, was to no avail, since his interrogator did not want to hear why he had published the article, rather who had paid him to destroy the reputation of the government. Habib exonerated all his colleagues and even the editor in chief, but this, too, was pointless.

On the fifth day he was subjected to barbaric torture. He collapsed, unconscious, and awakened in the cell, where his fellow inmates had forgotten their hatred and accepted him as one of them. They gave him cigarettes that had been smuggled in and told him why they were there.

Every party, profession, and ethnic group in Syria was represented in that cell. Among them was also a madman who had been called a spy. He continually sang sad songs about his sparrow, whose murderers he sought. Things went very badly for him, and after several days he became ill. But then something happened that greatly astonished the prisoners. A sparrow came flying, perched on the little windowsill, and trilled away as if possessed. At first the prisoners wanted to drive it off, but the madman was very happy about the bird and fed it with bread crumbs from his own mouth. Every day the sparrow came flying, but on the third day the madman was so sick he had to be moved. After that the sparrow vanished. I asked Habib to describe the man—I'm sure he was my madman.

When I was leaving, Habib said to me, "In this country no one can practice journalism." All he wants to do now is translate.

December 20 — Habib is diligently working away on his translation. He was in an excellent mood today, but when I asked again if he really wanted to give everything up because of his imprisonment, he screamed at me and tore off his shirt. Horrifying scars cover his entire chest!

"This is journalism!" he cried. I looked away. It hurt me. But he calmed down, and we laughed about the editor in chief, who now constantly apologizes on the radio and in the papers, in the hope of getting a job again.

I asked Habib if Nadia and I might come to his place once a week. He guffawed. "Once in seven days? Are you monks? You can come here seven times a day." He winked at me and nudged me in the side. Of course I have to tell Nadia about this right away.

December 23 — Habib and I have had another fight. I can't get it out of my head that one should be able to work as a journalist here even without the government newspaper. But Habib asked aggressively, "How then?" and I could not help myself; I screamed back, "If I had been a journalist as long as you, I would have found hundreds of ways." But he is stubborn and continues to enjoy translating the novel. Today he reproached me, calling me an incorrigible idiot. Let him say that. It doesn't offend me in the least.

The
Third
Year

January 11 — Today I saw the madman. They let him out of jail. He was squatting outside the Umayyad Mosque, mute as one of its stone pillars. People went by without paying him any mind, though now and then someone tossed him a coin.

I recognized him right away, even though he is greatly changed. His hair has been cut; his skin is very pale. Two round scars gleam from his temples; they look like they were burned in with two glowing metal rods. He sat entirely still. The pigeons, which enjoy special protection in the proximity of the mosque and thus fly around cooing in droves, don't interest him at all.

I squatted down beside him and started talking to him. He looked at me with wide eyes and repeated my question, "What's wrong with you, Uncle? What's wrong?" He rubbed his temples with his knotty fingers and began to cry. Then he gazed into the distance and was silent.

What horrifying torture this poor man must have endured. Out of a wise man they have made a miserable bundle of flesh and bones.

January 15 — Today I had an unpleasant row with Josef. From day to day he grows more enthusiastic about the army. He plans, because he is so big and strong, to join the paratroopers and go to war. I told him a joke I'd heard from Uncle Salim, who cannot tolerate any army on earth:

A parachutist is supposed to land behind enemy lines and carry out an act of sabotage. His commanding officer explains the delicate operation and how it should be accomplished: "Since your mission is very important, we have equipped you with a double parachute. After you've jumped, press the green button, and the chute will open. If it doesn't work, which seldom happens, press the red button. Then the second chute will open with one-hundred-percent certainty. When you land, you will find a motorbike leaning against a tree. Get on it and go to the rendezvous."

The paratrooper jumps. He presses the green button several times, but the chute doesn't open. "Okay," he says, and pushes the red button—once, twice—but the second chute doesn't open either. "This is not my day," he curses. "And when I land, I bet the motorcycle will have been stolen."

Josef didn't find the joke about the stupid paratrooper the least bit funny. He was annoyed and said that only cowards like myself and senile Uncle Salim could tell such jokes. That hurt me a lot.

January 20 — How can one publish a newspaper without the government banning it? Lots of underground parties print their own newspapers and then pass them from hand to hand. I've gotten copies of two such newspapers from acquaintances. They were one big yawn. Is it worth endangering your life for such imbecilic drivel? No!

Habib has left the ruling party. I share his happiness. Mariam and I had tea at his place. Eighteen years he was in the underground and suffered every disgrace because of his party. Once it came into power, he couldn't remain in it for even two years.

January 27 — We wanted to see another skin-flick. Mahmud arranged to get the tickets. This time I specifically wanted to seek out my math teacher and say hello to him, but he wasn't there, or at least I didn't see him.

Shortly before the film began, a man got up on the stage and loudly announced, "Unfortunately, we cannot show the film. The new chief of police has found out about it, and in half an hour he will send in plainclothesmen. If he catches us, he'll have the theater closed."

The lights went down, and suddenly a kitschy, schmaltzy film came on. The entire theater went wild, and somebody began to tear up the fine cloth of the lovely seats. Soon others started to jump up and rampage. Even Mahmud got out his pocket knife and slit the upholstery.

Amidst laughter and angry cries, the sweet dialogue of the schmaltzy film could be heard. We all laughed at the enamored hero, who had smeared a kilo of grease into his hair and was in a garden saying to his former lover, "I hover like a cloud when I see you. You and I, two flowers in the garden of love."

Amidst unanimous howling, someone cried out, "I will deliver some fertilizer to your garden! Right away!" When the owners finally understood and turned on the lights, the auditorium was one big rubbish dump.

They deserved it!

February 13 — Habib has changed somehow. He laughs a lot more and drinks less. He translates as if possessed. I brought him an exquisite meat pie that my mother made especially for him. But he won't talk about the paper.

Thursday — "How would you get a message or a story to a lot of people?" I asked Uncle Salim.

"I would take my whip and go to the radio station, fight my way through to the microphone, and say: 'Ladies and gentlemen, this is Salim the Coachman speaking to you. I want to tell you a story. Whoever does not wish to hear it can turn off the radio for five minutes, because I don't want to bore any of you—from old men to infants—as our president does.'"

"And what would you do when soldiers came while you were talking?" I laughed.

"Well, then everybody listening would experience real theater on the radio."

My dear uncle has not been outside our quarter for a long time. There are several panzer tanks outside the radio station. He wouldn't get very far with a whip.

February 19 — Habib gave me a fine shawl to take to my mother. She was delighted with the present. It had to be very expensive, she said, because its white wool comes from abroad. She said she'll drape it over her shoulders when she drinks her early-morning coffee on the terrace. My mother reciprocated with a small flask of orange-blossom oil she had distilled herself. Habib likes this scent very much.

February 27 — For two hours Habib made himself scarce so I could be with my Nadia in his apartment. Nadia was embarrassed about meeting Habib. We told each other our dreams. It was wonderful to be able to hold her in my arms.

I have written two poems about our secret trysts.

March 13 — Habib has gotten more translation jobs, two short crime stories and a thick novel. His publisher is enthusiastic about the good work he has turned in.

Now he seldom drinks, but he still smokes like a chimney. Last week my mother did Habib's laundry, and Mariam helps him somewhat with his household chores. He has two left hands and stumbles over things as if he had a third leg.

Unlike Habib, Uncle Salim does his laundry himself. Nor does he ever allow anyone to tidy up his room, not even when he's sick.

March 15 — I have the solution! Today I went back to the bazaar with my mother, and when she once again sat at one of the big merchants' booths, having offered less than half of the asking price, I meandered through the bustling stands. I knew my mother would buy the fabric; she had been talking about it for three days and pricing it with several different dealers. I knew that she and the merchant would come to terms somewhere in the middle of their price range but that it would take some time. I was right. Half an hour later I returned; the merchant was happily wrapping up the cloth for my mother. But something else I saw at the bazaar was more important than all the cloth in the world.

Some dealers are so poor that they don't even have their own booths. They transport their wares on carts or simply in big pieces of cloth and offer them for sale in the middle of the bazaar. The well-off merchants in the surrounding shops do not like this, but they allow it, primarily because the small dealers tend to sell third-rate goods for very little money.

"Socks thrown away! Socks given away!" a boy loudly cried.

A cluster of people immediately gathered round. On the cloth was an enormous heap of bright socks. People pushed and shoved because two pairs cost but one measly Syrian pound. I pressed forward and managed to pick out two pairs.

Once I got home, I wanted to try the socks on. They were held together with a simple clip. Instead of the transparent paper that is usually stuffed inside to help them keep their shape, the manufacturer of these third-rate socks had used ordinary shredded newspaper.

I let out a yelp of excitement, for I suddenly knew how to get a newspaper to other people quickly, distributing it without the government noticing a thing.

I hurried to Habib's, but the little red slip of paper was hanging on his door. (We use it when one of us is inside with his girlfriend, so the other won't come in. Nowadays I have my own key to his apartment.) I had forgotten that Mariam's husband had gone to Beirut for two days.

I'll tell Habib about it tomorrow.

March 16 — I told Mahmud about my idea, and he thought it was great. I wrote a rather long story on a narrow strip of paper and stuck it inside the socks. You can't see anything from outside.

"And what if people just throw the paper away?"

"They might do that. But as soon as word about the first sock-newspaper gets out, nobody will throw away the paper without reading it first."

Mahmud suggested we distribute the strips of paper

not only in socks, but everywhere—in public toilets and in cinemas. He told me that one day in the café he got to know an old author who had been in prison for many long years and had written an entire book on three hundred cigarette papers. He was even able to smuggle it out and get it published.

March 18 — First Habib laughed at me. I was fit to scream, but then he grew silent and began to pace back and forth, lost in thought. I told him that Mahmud and I wanted to sell the socks—quick as lightning and each time somewhere different, in and around Damascus.

"What will you do if they catch you?" he asked with concern.

"I'll go to prison like you, Father, and hundreds of others. But I want to be a journalist, to seek the truth and make it known."

Habib deliberated a while. He opened the door to his closet and gazed at the picture of his wife. Then I knew he would go along with it.

We continued to talk for a long time. Tomorrow I'll find out where the socks come from, and the day after that, we'll meet at Habib's.

March 19 — The cheap socks are manufactured at a small factory near the river. Four pairs cost one pound when you purchase in bulk, so we'll even make a nice profit.

Habib is writing an article about prison. I want to write about the madman of Damascus. For this madman could be any one of us, and his sparrow was his hope. What they did to him is what they plan to do to us all.

Mahmud arrived around eight. It was about time my best friends got to know each other. They had a lot of fun together, and later, on the way home, Mahmud told me that he thought Habib was very clever.

Habib wanted to call the newspaper *The Spark*, but Mahmud and I simply wanted to call it *Sock-Newspaper*; Habib agreed.

Habib asked Mahmud what he would write.

"Seven questions for every issue."

"Is this out of some fairy tale?"

"No, seven questions, one for each day." Mahmud gave some examples: "Have you ever seen the shabby hut of a minister?—Have you had enough to eat today?—Have you asked the president for permission to breathe?—Have you considered today how many kilos of bread a panzer tank costs?"

We didn't go home until late into the night. I have seldom felt as much strength as today, and Habib was never so childlike.

March 22 — Our street is supposed to be widened so that tourists' cars can drive down it. The residents don't like this idea, so they protested to the city council. In vain! This has been planned for fifteen years and will be carried out.

April 2 — Today Josef got hold of a book containing a few of the forbidden erotic tales from *The Thousand and One Nights*. He and Mahmud and I sat down together and read the slim volume with pleasure. But the chapter about the love potions and the techniques of lovemaking was so funny, we nearly laughed ourselves to death. No mere human being can concoct the salves. It went something like this: Take the shell of an eagle egg, fry it in the oil of the sacred tree, and store it all in a marble bowl for ninety-three days; knead into it one tablespoon of gum arabic while pronouncing an impossible charm. This paste must be left to draw on the leaf of an exotic tree for thirty-three days. Once this has been accomplished, place a tiny ball, the size of a lentil, into the coffee of your beloved; it will make him or her submissive.

At worst the techniques and postures themselves will result in bone fractures and muscle cramps. We joked about the idiots who had thought this stuff up.

"If I put one of these tiny balls into my girlfriend's coffee," Josef said, "she'll spit and say: 'Hey, old boy, can't you even make decent coffee? This tastes like the water your socks have been soaking in.'" She would leave him.

"And if before long I'm running around in a cast," Mahmud laughed, "and someone asks me, 'Have you had an accident?' tersely I'll reply, 'No, sex!'"

April 3 — Our articles were far too long; we had to cut them. Habib said this was the first time it was clear to him how important a single word could be. Mahmud has reformulated his questions even more wittily.

Two hundred pairs of socks wait in a carton at Habib's. He will get hold of a small, primitive duplicating machine. One of his old friends has long been working as a taxi driver on the route between Damascus and Beirut. In Beirut you can buy such a machine cheaply and quickly.

April 16 — Today Uncle Salim dined with us, and my father urged a third glass of *arrack* upon him. The old man became a bit tipsy and made terrific jokes. We all laughed so loud, people passing by on the street stopped in curiosity. When one man asked what it was we were celebrating, my father said, "The wedding day of our lice." The man laughed.

Uncle Salim asked the funniest question. "Why do many states have the eagle—an idiotic animal—on their flags?"

"They want to instill courage in us," my father answered, chuckling. "They know we are timid, and they think: Tell the pigeon three times it is an eagle, and just wait and see; it will start to hunt mice."

"But an eagle will even eat carrion when it has to. *Igitt, igitt!* It's coming, it's coming! Our government knows us but poorly. I'll just have to look up the president and suggest that they paint a goat on our flags. Goats are more like us."

"Because they bleat and moan or because they don't eat any meat?"

"Neither. Because they get milked!" Uncle Salim laughed.

April 20 — The mimeograph machine has arrived. Habib showed us how to use stencils. The copies are in violet ink, but they're easy to read. We folded the strips and stuffed them into the socks. Habib's article is amazing. My piece about the madman also pleased him and Mahmud. Mahmud's seven questions are fabulous.

April 23 — Habib took the cinemas, restaurants, and cafés (two hundred of them); Mahmud and I went to the bazaar. One of us kept watch and the other did the selling. I spread out the big cloth and began to cry "Socks," and in half an hour they were gone. Then we hurried our separate ways back to our jobs because lunch break was over.

Habib was very relieved when we turned up at his

place toward seven o'clock. He served us cakes and made excellent tea. We had our own cigarettes.

April 26 — I was against it, but Mahmud wanted to assure himself. Today he went to see Josef and told him that he had a friend who had given him a copy of the sock-newspaper. Mahmud asked Josef if he wanted to read it and pass a copy on. According to Mahmud, Josef went dead white and spoke softly, as if afraid someone might overhear. He is just about to take his final exams and then wants to go straight into the army. He has no interest in newspapers, and none whatsoever in those who write against the government. He doesn't want to have anything to do with something like that, and when he's a general, he himself will stage a coup.

Saturday — Four days later, during lunch break, my boss told us a customer had given him a remarkable newspaper. He praised the questions and said that all night long he had lain awake contemplating his life. He admired the courage of the underground group and wished he could support it somehow.

May 20 — For three weeks our street has looked gruesome. The houses opposite ours have lost eight meters in depth. Their façades have been cut off. Many small houses have vanished; others, owing to the severing, have become narrow and ugly. We are choking in exhaust fumes and dust. The bulldozers make a hellish noise. The workmen get started very early because they cannot work in the heat of midday; then they resume and work into the night.

We have lost many neighbors. I am sad that Josef and his mother had to move to a street far away. Only three dark rooms remain of what once was their big building; Josef's uncle lives there because he cannot afford a better apartment. Thank God Mahmud and Nadia are still here. For centuries people have lived here, and now these small clay houses crumble to dust within days. They are no match for the bulldozers.

May 25 — Today began like a dream. I awakened at dawn, smelling jasmine right near my bed. I went out on the terrace and saw hundreds of flowers open their calyxes in the cool morning dew. Without the fourteen children who run wild during the day, our courtyard seemed much bigger.

Tuesday — Today, two weeks later, even BBC London is talking about our sock-newspaper. Extracts from my article and the whole of Habib's were read aloud, but, strangely enough, not a single one of Mahmud's questions was mentioned.

June 10 — How Mahmud comes up with his ideas and writes them all out so brilliantly in just a couple of pages is a mystery to me. I am extremely proud of him. Today he finished his third play; it's even better than the first two:
A man is insulted and beaten by an officer. At the police station he gets more of the same. The testimony of an officer carries more weight than that of a poor, tattered devil. And so the man decides to get himself a uniform, and onto its shoulder he pins a couple of stars—which can be bought anywhere. He shaves and moves into a small room in another part of town. From that time on, the man embarks upon a new life.

During the day he practices his trade, and in the evening he walks around in uniform, enjoying the salutes of the soldiers. A few days later he promotes himself to the rank of general. Now the jeeps of the military police also leave him alone, and he feels even better because many plainclothes policemen greet him and smile. He even goes to restaurants, has meals, and writes bad checks, signing himself as a general. Every day he turns up on a different street. One day he happens upon a coup and gets involved, keeping a clear head amidst the confusion and giving intelligent orders. The coup founders, and he saves the existing government. The play is like a fairy tale and concludes with the question of whether our own government isn't made up of such people.

June 26 — For the first time the official newspaper has taken a stand. A band of agents, in the pay of Israel, is making trouble in our country, seeking to weaken our unity. The government is threatening "to strike with an iron hand."

Habib laughed and said, "First the iron will have to be imported!"

July 5 — A new language has been evolving on our street since it was widened. The old expressions, "Go play in the street," "You can do that outside on the street," and "You are not on the street, where you can play as you like," are gone forever. The new street sayings are: "Look out for cars!," "Better play here in the apartment," and "Anywhere but in the street; you could lose your skin there."

Our mothers are having trouble adjusting. Sometimes one of them will say, irritably, "Go outside!" But then she'll quickly correct herself and say, "I mean, settle down."

Writing these lines has made me think of Robert. Our streets are slowly beginning to resemble those he described, but here we still don't have as much to eat as they do in Europe.

July 10 — "Today it's my treat. Are you in the mood to hear tall tales?"

No question about that! Of course I was in the mood, and together we set out. Uncle Salim knows half the town. Again and again he stopped to greet merchants and craftsmen. When we reached a certain coffeehouse, Uncle Salim was disappointed. The old storyteller had died, and no one had taken his place. He asked if there was anywhere else to go to hear someone tell tales. We learned there still are a few such cafés. The best-known one is near the Umayyad Mosque.

And so we strolled there. The café was rather full. Many tourists were waiting and drinking tea. We sat down near the high stool of the storyteller. Toward seven o'clock he arrived. He spoke quite loudly and always made lively gestures with his hands to accentuate danger or intensify battles. The tourists photographed him, and he grew louder and wilder. This pleased some members of the audience, and at the tops of their lungs they interjected their remarks. The storyteller recounted the fight between two clans, and after a while two men in the room were fighting, because each of them favored a different side. The customers sitting nearby calmed them down.

The storyteller recited in verse what the adversaries said to each other. Each praised himself to the skies and boundlessly reproached his enemy. At times it was funny. I laughed when one hero glorified not only his sword, his horse, and his own poetic talents, but even his mustache, saying, "My mustache is so strong, a falcon can perch on it." A guest with an immense mustache glared at me angrily from a neighboring table and twirled his magnificent handlebars.

Just when the tale was most thrilling, the storyteller broke off. He asked those present to return to the coffeehouse the next day, when he would continue the saga of the hero, who was about to saw through the bars of his prison window.

Uncle Salim was visibly disappointed. "Like bread, storytellers are getting worse and worse," he complained after a while. "He bellows and waves his hands about, but his voice does not stir the heart. A storyteller must speak softly; the softer he is, the wiser he is."

I defended the storyteller, saying he had to bellow in order to be heard, but I didn't convince Uncle Salim. "A bad storyteller laughs at his own joke before he has finished telling it."

He's right. Sometimes the man laughed out loud and said, "Here comes the funny part." But what followed was more likely to be sad or sometimes dull.

July 11 — Uncle Salim is enthusiastic about the paper. He suspects his friend the old journalist is behind it. I have long contemplated telling him, but I will not say a word. This secret is mine alone.

July 12 — I have asked Nadia to ask her boss whether it is possible to take legal action against the editor Ahmad Malas because of the radio play. It was some time ago, but who knows?

July 14 — Nadia said her boss doesn't believe that this play—which meanwhile has become very famous—came from the pen of a fifteen-year-old. Moreover, Malas has been the darling of every government and has become a powerful editor. "The testimony of fifty children isn't worth a piece of crap." (Nadia swore these were his exact words.) Malas can at any time prove that he and not Mahmud wrote and broadcast the play years ago. Is that what is commonly called justice?

July 16 — I have spoken with Habib. He knows Ahmad Malas. "All these characters live off the work of others. It would be interesting to write an article showing just how much many famous poets and musicians have stolen." When he does this, he will also take up Mahmud's case.

July 18 — Habib is a different person. He sings constantly and is very cheerful.

Lots of people continue to talk about the sock-newspaper, even though a month has gone by. I have the feeling many people are making copies and passing it along. They say it has turned up in Aleppo and in Homs. I have learned from Nadia that the secret service is really spinning its wheels.

During lunch break I have begun to learn how to type. My boss is griping about it a little. He fears for his typewriter. Sometimes I can't find a letter at all; it's as if it were hiding from my blows.

July 22 — Nadia came to Habib's apartment for an hour today. She'll soon be sixteen and no longer a child. In the last months she has grown quickly. We love each other very much, and we often talk about the future. Today I nearly put my foot in my mouth. When I was discussing our prospective children, I said, ". . . who hopefully will have no need of a sock-newspaper." Nadia looked at me wide-eyed, and I tried to play this down by making a joke of it. "I mean," I retorted, "the state newspaper, which stinks like sweaty socks."

Nadia shook her head. "Your jokes are getting sillier and sillier," she said, and buttoned up her blouse.

July 24 — Not long ago I wrote two poems. The first was about the women poets praise until they marry; once they marry, they forget their songs and torment their wives. The second was about the sea, which exerts itself, leaping up to wash away the clouds from the face of the sky because it misses the blue color.

August 1 — Habib is nearly finished with his translation. Today he got an advance and made dinner at his place for Mahmud and me. (Mariam looked in briefly.) I bragged that I could type two pages an hour. In reality all I can do is one, and that one with lots of errors.

In the bookshop, my boss let me type a few letters. Today I typed "Dear Mr. Hound" instead of "Dear Mr. Pound." Thank God my boss checked the letter. Then he said, "If I want to put Mr. Pound off, all I have to do is tell you to write him a letter. For then he will be Dearest Hound, and the book he ordered wasn't on swans but swines, and our Kindest wishes will become our Blindest fishes."

August 3 — The second issue is ready! I have typed quite a lot. Habib wrote about corruption. He condoned the bribe-taking of petty officials who need the money to feed their children, but attacked the venality of the ministers who are bleeding the country.

I also wrote about the poor students who, at too young an age, have to leave school and go to work.

Again Mahmud thought up really great questions. The first one was: "Have you already read the first issue of the sock-newspaper?"

We urged all people fortunate enough to have learned to read and write to make their own newspapers. Habib came up with a lovely sentence: "Communication is the responsibility of every human being; don't leave it to the government!"

Sunday — We have run off six hundred copies. On Friday Mahmud and I carried the socks to the marketplace; again they sold in a flash. Then we walked through the bazaar and looked at the stands. We saw a man with a dancing bear—a piteous animal, emaciated and sad, its body covered with scars. It hobbled around, and Mahmud said he was sure the bear was crying and that bears, like people, understand everything. How humiliating this dance would be if the bear really has feelings as we do.

August 6 — Today Uncle Salim told me the story of a sultan who, on an outing, came upon a picturesque village and wanted to stop and rest there. He dismounted from his horse, and the peasants threw their jackets under his feet so his shoes would not get dusty. They were delighted because he was the first ruler ever to visit their village.

A huge table was conjured forth and set up on the village square. Immediately a great feast was prepared: mutton stuffed with almonds, raisins, and rice; salad; cheese; wine. The sultan was amazed at the people's wealth and exclaimed loudly that their harvest tax would be doubled. Then he began to eat. He ate like a bull, wheezing, belching, and gorging himself.

Suddenly the sultan felt tired. He looked all around and announced to his soldiers, "No one may leave the table before I awaken." The soldiers drew their swords and held the men in check. The sultan snored away. Night fell. The men grew weary, but the soldiers changed watch and commanded those present to remain at the table. The sultan went on sleeping blissfully. Morning came; the men were faint with fatigue, but the sultan still dozed. At noon he finally woke up in a bad mood, with a stiff neck. He cursed the village in which a guest could not even get a soft bed; then he rode off.

Since that day the peasants no longer lay their jackets at a visitor's feet. Instead, they are suspicious and sometimes throw stones at him to send him on his way.

August 8 — Radio Israel, Radio Jordan, and BBC London have reported on the second edition of our newspaper. Habib said that in the third issue he will settle up with all the various parties; he will show that in Syria there is no opposition among them. We also decided, beginning with that issue, to run a small literary column.

August 12 — Uncle Salim and my father have become enthusiastic followers of the newspaper. My father listens to BBC London and was very taken with the third question: "Do you happen to know how many days a week a baker works? (The answer is seven, because bakers, despite a decades-long battle, still don't have a day off.) And how many days in his life does a big landowner work? (The answer is approximately zero.)"

August 17 — Damascus is most beautiful at dawn. Today I awakened from a dream and crept out of my room onto the terrace. The street sweepers had just finished up on our street. They shouldered their long brooms and walked home with slow strides. They looked tired. I had an idea about what street sweepers and bakers have in common, but now, in the afternoon, I can't think what it was.

August 18 — Somehow or other the paper has changed me. I look at things more carefully, and when I see or hear something, questions more than answers rise up in me. I also love Nadia very much, and I'm certain we belong together. This gives me peace of mind.

When I read my early diary entries today, I was ashamed. I would have liked to tear them out. But I have sworn not to alter anything, so all of it will remain. There was much I would have forgotten if I had not immediately made my notes. I have also become far more diligent. Whether I'm content, sad, or indifferent, I write it down. Habib already has more than ten volumes in all.

August 20 — Last night I sat long on the terrace, looking at the stars. I wanted to write a poem about the night, but my thoughts kept straying and ended up with Nadia. If only she could lie beside me for a few moments, and in the freshness of the night we could gaze at the stars together!

A few days ago Nadia said to me, "Sometimes I wish your head lay on my pillow so we could share the same dream."

I have no further wishes anymore.

August 21 — The third issue went off very smoothly today. It is even more readable than the first two. Mahmud's questions and my story about the cunning inhabitants of Homs, who for centuries have affected lunacy, worked out well.

The owner of the sock factory suspiciously asked us our names and where we lived. Of course we made something up, but we have to be careful. The secret service has been getting very sharp. Habib is extraordinarily fearful for us.

August 24 — Today we had a close call. I spread out my cloth in front of a cinema in the new quarter. The cheap socks attracted passersby, and within a short time I had sold three-quarters of our wares. Mahmud kept a lookout nearby. Suddenly a well-dressed man tore open a package of socks and grabbed me by the collar. Mahmud noticed this and, like greased lightning, rammed into the man so forcefully from behind that he toppled over and hit the ground. I slipped out of his grip and ran as fast as I could. The man screamed, "Stop! Thief! Stop! Thief!" in the hope that passersby would help, but no one did.

As I scaled a wall and ran down an alley on the other side, children playing with marbles cried out in terror. A woman gazing out a window called to her neighbor, "Just look how pale the poor boy is!"

As I came to a busy street, I put on the brakes, slowing my pace. I walked into the first café I saw and ordered a lemonade. I had to sit for half an hour before I felt strength in my knees again. My boss was grouchy, but he's been like that a lot lately. The bookshop is not doing so well. We have competition.

Habib was utterly appalled and proud at the same

time. He said we have to find a new way, always look for new ways, and not use the same ones too long. In Aleppo, he learned through a friend, three groups also producing sock-newspapers have been caught.

August 27 — Neither the Israeli nor the Jordanian broadcasters have said a word about our third edition, even though (thanks to Habib's courage—he stuffed the paper into over three hundred mailboxes) it was far more widely distributed. Habib said they probably were keeping silent so the disgruntled masses in other countries would not make their own sock-newspapers.

There must still be some other clever way!

August 29 — Nadia asked me why I've been so aggressive lately. I'm sorry I can't tell her, but I don't want to put her in jeopardy.

September 1 — A coup! Once again the new government, composed of old generals, has discovered that the preceding regime consisted of nothing but thieves and traitors. This isn't even funny!

The prisons are overflowing, and Nadia's father serves the new government as a spy. He has just removed the photo of the old president from their living room and is waiting for the new president to have his picture taken.

September 2 — Habib has a new idea. He has given a great deal of thought to which cheap, salable articles are packed in paper. Oranges are extremely well suited to our purpose; the newspaper strips could easily be hidden beneath the bright paper they are wrapped in. We've completely rejected textiles because it takes too long to get them to consumers. Habib has been working as a day laborer in the packing department of a pharmaceutical firm. They manufacture only a few items (headache pills and the like), but they do so by the ton. He could slip our newspaper into the packages with the tablets. The firm is near Damascus; the oranges are packed on the coast, but Habib will drive there.

September 4 — Habib forges like a pro. He magically made himself a set of identity papers with an assumed name.

I have an idea about how we can bring the paper to people everywhere. A balloon filled with a light gas could hold several strips inside; when it bursts somewhere in the sky, the strips will fall over the city. Mahmud is enthusiastic about the idea and reminded me about the experiment we made with hydrogen in school. A little zinc and hydrochloric acid will release hydrogen. Tomorrow we're going to try it.

September 5 — Today we opened our witches' kitchen in the attic. A soda bottle, a few pieces of zinc (from a broken gutter), and hydrochloric acid (it's called spirit of salt in the shop and is quite cheap) were all we needed. The contents of the bottle foamed and seethed, and when we set a match to the gas, a bluish flame hissed up and scared us. The bottle tipped over, and the mixture ate into the wooden floor and smelled awful. We coughed like maniacs! But then we managed to fill a balloon with the gas, and it rose in the sky rather quickly.

How will we get it to the height at which it will burst? If we can't, only God above will be able to read the strips of paper in the belly of the balloon. Maybe we should fasten a long string to it and light the string? We tried this with the next balloon, but the string didn't burn. Tomorrow we will drench it in diesel oil.

September 8 — Darkness was upon the fields on the outskirts of Damascus. Mahmud stuffed thirty newspaper strips into a big balloon and filled it with gas. I dipped its thin string in diesel oil, and we let the balloon go up. When it reached a height of about ten meters in the dark sky, we lit the string. But the flames raced up too quickly, and before the balloon could rise a few meters more, there was a dreadful bang.

We ran away quickly. We took the bottle and the remains of the zinc with us. On our way we encountered people gazing skyward in confusion, talking about the explosion. Suddenly Mahmud began to laugh. He is quite a guy! In the midst of every catastrophe he finds something to laugh about. At first I was annoyed, but then I joined in his crazy laughter, and we were delighted by the agitated people who suspected they'd seen a UFO. They'll discover the pages soon enough. Now the newspaper has a cosmic collaborator.

September 11 — I have saved one hundred and eighty-six pounds. When I have two hundred altogether, I will buy my mother a dress that costs fifty.

Things are going somewhat better in the bookstore, and my boss isn't grumbling so often. Now he has a few titles that are hits with university students: *200 Questions Pertaining to Medicine*, *300 Questions Pertaining to Chemistry*, *150 Questions Pertaining to Law*. Students buy these brochures as if possessed, and the profit per pamphlet is not thirty but fifty percent. And just look at our future doctors, chemists, and lawyers! They read the questions, learn the answers like parrots, and spit them out on paper. In olden times a medicine man or medicine woman was a wise person. When I read about everything that one Avicenna or a single Leonardo da Vinci knew, the university and its teachers seem pathetic.

Yesterday Habib said that Socrates had not read more books in his lifetime than a person who nowadays has taken his university entrance exam, but that with his knowledge Socrates reached even to the root of life. I don't know anything at all about Socrates. Today I looked around in the shop. There are three books about him.

September 13 — We nearly burned up the attic experimenting with the string and diesel oil. With my face entirely black, I went into the kitchen. My mother made fun of me. All evening she called me chimney sweep, and finally my father wanted to know why. She fibbed, saying that I'd gotten dirty helping her in the kitchen.

This is something I especially love about my crazy mother. She never tells on us. Even when we've nearly driven her nuts, she settles things with us herself. She never says, "Just wait until your father gets home." Sometimes she hits us, crying while she does; then we, too, keep our mouths shut when my old man returns. Mahmud's mother always runs right to his father and gripes about one thing or another. That's something I don't like about her.

September 14 — "Have you told Mariam about the newspaper?" I asked Habib.

"Of course I have. I don't want to make the same mistake twice." He told me how he had made a secret of his political work, hiding it from his wife out of concern for her. But his seeming prudence had not saved her. He had also seen how wives had unwittingly divulged the names of their husbands' friends, not knowing that these alleged merchants and docents, farmers and artisans, whom their husbands visited from time to time, were high-ranking functionaries. And so, by not having trusted their wives, having shared their beds only and let them cook, the men had betrayed their confidants. "Among spies I could understand this, but nowhere else!" he said.

I must talk to Nadia about this as soon as possible. I'm no spy!

September 16 — Habib packs up the orders for pharmacies in the factory storeroom. A tedious job. While doing it, he stuffs the newspaper strips into the boxes. We told him about our balloon, and he laughed until tears rolled down his cheeks.

September 18 — I haven't been to church in ages. My father asked me why, and I said I probably didn't go because I no longer needed pocket money. He almost choked with laughter. Uncle Salim, who had been listening with amusement to our conversation, told us a story:

"A poor man was out of work. He was very pious and always went to church; he prayed and prayed but found no work. One day he noticed that the collection box under the portrait of the Virgin Mary was full of coins and bills, but the box under the picture of Jesus was almost always empty.

"Soon after, the man had had his fill of begging. He entered the church, stood before the picture of the Virgin, and spoke to her.

" 'Blessed Mary, all day long I seek work and do not

find it. My children need their food and clothing and I my schnapps, but, as you see, I haven't got a single cent. I'm not a bad person. Just look at your son's box. Nothing. The wind whistles in it. And he's not bad either. May I take twenty pounds? I will share it with your son, ten for me and ten for him. My children will get their food and I my schnapps. It will stand your son in good stead, too. If you don't want me to do this, just say so, and I won't even lay a finger on it.'

"Of course the picture made no reply, and the man did as he said. The next day he came back.

"'O holy Virgin, I am so ashamed,' he said, 'I cannot even look you in the eye. But what should I do? Look, things go no better for your son. Not a single piaster. Today I need forty pounds, for the rent is due. But I am like a camel; I forget nothing. I will also give forty to your son. If this is too much, just say so. I won't touch a thing.' Naturally the image didn't say a word, and the man took eighty pounds from the overstuffed box, divided them, and went his way.

"The man's situation did not improve in the following days, and he came, took, and divided. But he always asked whether the Virgin had any objection; she never did.

"The priest puzzled a long time over this sudden change in the two collection boxes. In ten years he had never seen such paltry figures for Mary and such good ones for Jesus. Suddenly his accounts no longer balanced, and to find out the reason, he hid behind the painting of Jesus and waited.

"The man came in, eyes to the ground, and said, 'O Blessed Virgin, for two weeks I have been searching for work and finding none. I told my wife and children they have your good heart to thank for all I have given them, and every day they pray for you. Before, my wife couldn't stand you, but now you can count on her in hard times. I seem to be saying a lot today because the rent must be paid again, and I'm ashamed. But the woodworms in your son's box are catching cold from the draft. Still, if you don't want me to, just say so, and I'll leave everything as it is.'

" 'No, I don't want you to!' the priest cried out in anger.

"Infuriated, the man turned to the picture of Jesus. 'Shut your trap. I'm talking to your mother! But very well, if you don't want me to, I won't share with you any longer,' he scolded, took the eighty pounds, and left."

The most wonderful thing is how Uncle Salim manages to extract from his memory the right story for every occasion.

September 20 — A splendid day! Today I went to the circus with Nadia. The afternoon show began at three. An impoverished troupe from India is visiting the exhibition center. They don't even have a cash register; a man just stands there collecting money. With his scant knowledge of Arabic, he has a lot of trouble doing his job, and all the spectators seem to want to haggle.

During the performance nothing went right. The dogs refused to jump through the fiery hoops and raced under them instead. The elephants had diarrhea. The tightrope walker slipped even after his fifth attempt; the rope, however, was only about two meters off the ground.

The master of ceremonies tried hard to introduce the tiger act in an interesting way. "A matter of life and death!" he cried. The tigers slinked around inside the ring, yawning incessantly, then fell asleep. The tamer roared at them like a lion, but the big cats each sleepily opened one eye and went on yawning. The children laughed heartily.

The knife-throwing number, thank God, was the one thing that went smoothly. Upset, Nadia closed her eyes and pressed my hand. I found the act abominable. The poor girl who stood there trembling was as beautiful as a rose.

The loveliest act was that of the sad clown. He told a love story without saying a word. All he had was a withered flower that he took great pains to bring back to life. The spectators howled, but Nadia and I wept.

October 1 — We have solved the problem of the string. After days filled with tears and coughing, we realized that a few drops of diesel oil were enough to make the cord burn slowly but surely.

From atop the roof of an old abandoned factory, we sent up a big balloon with fifty strips inside. The wind carried it over the inner city. Suddenly it blazed up blue in the dark sky. We waited a moment, stashed the bag with our chemical laboratory in a rusty barrel, and hurried home.

October 15 — Habib ran off another three hundred strips of the fourth issue. He gave notice at the pharmaceutical firm, and tomorrow he is going north to work as an orange packer.

By hand he added a note in French: *Show this strip to an Arab and let him translate what it says for you. We would be thankful if you would then pass our newspaper on to a journalist.*

Hopefully nothing will happen to him. A gutsy guy!

October 18 — How stupid we are despite all! The simplest solution was right under our noses, and we took tremendous detours, perilous detours, and inhaled soot and oil. All this was completely unnecessary. Today we came upon the idea that solved the problem. We filled a small, lightweight raffia basket with the leaflets, fastened it to the balloon, and sent it up. After a few meters, the wind blew the flyers out of the swinging basket. The lighter the load, the faster the balloon rose and dumped it. The wind distributed the papers for us. No more lightning and diesel fuel. So now it's also a little less dangerous.

November 6 — Three weeks have gone by and Habib is still up north. Nadia and I can meet more often. Best of all is when we make love at Habib's.

November 8 — I have been looking for the madman. I don't know why, but yesterday I dreamed about him. He is no longer at the entrance to the Umayyad Mosque. A perfume seller, who offers little aromatic flasks on a table there, told me the madman had grown weaker day by day and one day lay there unconscious. An ambulance picked him up, and since then he has not appeared again.

November 15 — Did I ever have a terrifying nightmare tonight! Habib squatted in front of the mosque with his mouth sealed shut. He had burns on his hands. They were square and red.

November 17 — Uncle Salim wanted to pour me some tea. His trembling hands could not hold the glass. It fell tinkling to the floor and shattered. I tried to make light of it, but Uncle Salim laughed at my concern.

"My friend, you have seen some of nature's wisdom and endeavor to excuse it." While we drank, he explained. "Nature, my friend, nature is mute. But she shows what she wants to say. Now she is telling me: Don't hold on tight to worldly things. You cannot take them along with you, and the more tightly you hold on to them, the faster they will slip through your fingers. That's what Nature says; she weakens the hands of old people so they can grasp and enjoy life more intensely than ever."

November 24 — After forty days, Habib has returned. Now he has a gray beard. The radio stations are talking about the fourth issue again. Habib hopes the oranges will soon come into good hands. He told us a lot about the sea and the fishermen.

December 23 — (Have written nothing for nearly a month!) What luck! In Marseille several people who bought oranges passed the strips on to journalists. Habib learned of this through a colleague and had a taxi driver bring a copy of the French newspaper, *Le Monde*, from Beirut. The Syrian government has banned this edition. They do this whenever there's anything at all against them in a newspaper. It's idiotic that everybody else knows things are going badly for us, while we alone are not allowed to learn about it.

This evening we all sat round the French newspaper, which displayed an illustration of the sock-newspaper beside a translation. Habib read us the introduction aloud. A more concise and exact report could not have been written. Both the socks and the balloons were mentioned; above all, they said the sock-newspaper was the only good paper in Syria.

Habib embraced me. "We have you and your pigheadedness to thank for this!" he said.

I nearly jumped for joy. The praise was too much for me, but now for the first time I can write: I AM A JOURNALIST!

P.S.: Habib said that *Le Monde* is read in many countries throughout the world.

The
Fourth
Year

January 2 — I had a second piece of good news today. In the forty days Habib was gone he translated a crime novel. The author's name is Maurice Leblanc, and the novel is one of twelve in an adventure series whose protagonist is a funny, brave thief named Arsène Lupin. The story is great, and even the author's life is an adventure. The thief can transform himself into different shapes incredibly quickly. He steals from the rich (good!!!) and gives to the poor. Not only the police but also his colleagues are after him because he snatches the loot away from them. He does all this without firing a shot; his clever head is superior to force. Habib says that Lupin is very much loved in France.

January 10 — Damn it! Mahmud is out of a job again. His boss had to give up. No one comes to him to have his clothes tailor-made anymore. People buy cheap, disposable goods and thus many small shops go under.

Although I offered him money, this time Mahmud did not want to make a secret of it at home. "No, he ought to know. I don't care whether he gets angry or not."

His father became raging mad, but Mahmud screamed back at him that he had lost the job not because he was bad, rather because the country was.

His father became quiet and made tea for Mahmud.

January 15 — Mahmud spent the whole day looking for a job. During lunch break I went round to some of our customers who are fond of me and asked whether they might need anybody. All of them were friendly, but nobody wanted help. What a shitty life, always having to look for work!

January 18 — I am writing many poems and short tales again. Nadia thinks they're lovely. Today I began a story about a very small red flower that attempts to climb over a huge stone because it doesn't believe the stone is the end of the world. I don't know what will happen to the flower.

Leila says my tales are odd. She would rather I write about marriages of princesses or princes. What do I care whether these sorts marry? I love Nadia and she is my red flower.

January 23 — Today I am seventeen. I hadn't given it any thought, but Habib absolutely insisted that Mahmud and I come to dinner. When I arrived, the superbly spread table was a surprise. Even Mariam joined us for half an hour.

January 30 — Today Nadia told me that her father talks about nothing but the newspaper. Swearing her to secrecy, I confessed that I and my friends made the newspaper. She swore by her love for me that she would rather die than betray me. But she did not believe me, for when leaving, she said, laughing, that the fairy tale about the newspaper was terrific.

I have written more of "The Red Flower." The flower climbs and climbs, surmounts the stone, and sees a vast world before it. It plays with the sun and falls in love with the moon, which tells it stories. Then a wind comes and brushes against the flower, wanting to glide over the stone. The wind flatters the flower and asks it to adapt itself, to cling to the stone like ivy.

Will the flower do it? What will happen if it doesn't?

February 6 — Uncle Salim dreamed of his dead wife today. She was naked and as young as on their first night. She took him into her soft arms, and he felt the pleasure of physical love as he had not in twenty years. Fabulous!

February 11 — Our neighbor the greengrocer had bad luck today, though at first it appeared to be good. This morning his wife brought his son into the world. The first son after seven daughters! He was so happy that he drank half a liter of *arrack* in the morning and soon was pleasantly drunk; toward noon he was dead drunk. He began to give away his produce, simply throwing it to passersby. A few poor devils gathered up carrots, tomatoes, and potatoes and hurried home before the stingy merchant came to his senses and demanded money for them. But others cursed him, because he'd hit them in the head with some vegetable. His joy grew and grew, as did the heap of vegetables he had cast around himself in his enthusiasm; for the first time in his life, he was the center of attention on the street.

But a melon put an end to the fun. An officer was strolling by, and it hit him solidly in the stomach. He staggered and fell into a puddle. The greengrocer's gaiety was contagious; a couple of hooligans, who had seldom seen an officer sitting in a puddle, rolled him in the mire and repeatedly tossed his cap in the air. The good luck turned to bad. Officers set great store by their uniforms. The greengrocer was taken to the police station, where he received a few blows and a fine, which hurt him even more.

February 20 — I am seventeen and still love the stories of my best friend Uncle Salim just as much as I did ten years ago. Today I think he has been very wise to repeat the stories at intervals, for not only do the stories change with the telling, but the listener also has grown older and carries away different "magic fruits" from each telling.

Stories are magical springs that never dry up.

March 1 — I told Mahmud and Habib that I had revealed everything to Nadia. They were not angry, as I had feared they would be. On the contrary! . . .

The red flower decides not to obey the wind and declines its seductive offers. The wind grows angry, turns into a storm, and attacks the flower. The red flower fights, striking back with its thorns, but is torn out and thrown to the ground. The other little flowers are afraid, and a few that wanted to dare climbing over the stone are disheartened. Some of the older flowers say, "That red flower had it coming, always so curious!" But the red flower replies by gently describing the world on the other side of the stone, speaking of the moon and the sun. Because until now all they knew was that the world consisted of moist earth and a huge stone, behind which some sort of twilight appeared. When the other flowers heard the red flower's tales, they began to climb. Many fell back, but others went forward. Since that day, there are no flowers behind the stone. They climb until they can see the sun and hear the moon's stories.

Nadia wept when I told her the tale. She said the flower could be any woman.

Leila did not like the story. She moaned that it would be better if the stupid wind died or got punched in the jaw. Her idea isn't so dumb. Maybe I'll settle up with the wind in another chapter.

March 11 — Mahmud has found a job washing dishes in a posh nightclub. I am against his working among pimps, as are Nadia and Mariam. Only Uncle Salim and Habib think no harm will come of it. To each his own. Uncle Salim said a lion would not become a dog if it gnawed a bone out of hunger. Habib also defended Mahmud, saying Mahmud had to earn his living and my screwed-up morals were useless for that. His remark really made me mad!

Mahmud was furious with me, and for the first time we really had a fight.

"You should become a priest and not a journalist," he said angrily. He was extremely snide, and I gave it back to him. "Better to be a priest than to earn one's living off whores!" I cried.

Habib defended the whores, saying they were just as good as ministers or housewives, no better and no worse. They have to get through somehow, too. "The state is the pimp!" he screamed and laughed peculiarly. "And you are a priest."

I ran out of the apartment in a rage. Mahmud followed me, and we walked home, not speaking. Shortly before we reached the door to the house, he grabbed hold of me. "You're my friend, even if you've hurt me," he said.

I embraced him and asked his forgiveness. But I don't want to go to Habib's anymore.

March 15 — "For the third time my wife has appeared to me in a dream. Over and over again she says she would like to see me soon," Uncle Salim stated, making me anxious. My mother believes in it. I'm worried about my friend, even though he is the picture of health.

March 19 — "You are my best friend. What a pity you were born so late. I would have liked to meet you sometime as a young coachman," Uncle Salim said today for no reason. I had dropped by to see if he needed anything from the market. All the children in the house do this. "Up until now my wife alone has seen my treasure," he went on, "but I want to show it to you as well; only afterward you must grant me a wish!" Salim took a small cigar box out from under the bed. He stroked it gently, as if it were made of silver. Carefully he opened it.

"Do you see this key?" he asked. "This is the key to my coach. I had to sell everything, but I would not hand over the key." He put it aside and took a marble out of the box. "I played with this marble as a child. It was my favorite, and when I rubbed it, it brought me luck in the game."

Then he took a small dried root out of his treasure chest. "This root is from a plant that grows in the mountains, where I hid myself. The plant is cut every year, and it always grows back. It cannot be killed. The peasants carry it in their pockets because it gives life. During my five-year flight I always had it with me. —And this gold coin is from a robber whose life I once saved. He gave me the task of giving it to someone who no longer sees any way out. I realized only very late how much wisdom was concealed in this robber, for whenever I wanted to give it to someone, we looked for a way and found one, too."

Uncle Salim was quiet for a long time, as if he surmised the great burden of his wish. "My friend," he finally said, "I would like you to lay the marble, the key, and the root in my grave with me. The gold coin I turn over to you with the robber's request."

I felt bad. "You are not going to die," I whispered hoarsely, but Uncle Salim insisted on giving me the box. Now it lies hidden under the boards in my closet, right where I keep my journal.

March 20 — Uncle Salim is sick. I brought him food and tea in bed. He's breathing heavily and says he caught cold from a draft.

P.S.: I have not been to Habib's for nine days.

March 21 — Late yesterday my mother came into my room and said there was a man downstairs at the door, asking for me. She suspected it was Habib because she recognized his shirt and trousers from having washed them.

I jumped out of bed. He was already standing there smiling. I invited him to come in. My mother hurried off to make coffee.

"I want to apologize to you. I was very rough on you, but you were impossible!" he said and ran his hand through my hair.

"Let's not start again. I only stated my opinion," I replied.

We talked and talked. He held to his position, as I did to mine, but he was polite. My mother brought the coffee and sat down with us.

"What a beautiful mother you have," the rogue flattered her; my mother laughed. We agreed I should come to his place today after work.

I went there today, as did Mahmud. His job doesn't begin until eight and goes on until four in the morning. He talked about it. The owner is a swine, and Mahmud's fondest wish is to smash him against a wall; still, the dancers and the hostesses are very nice. Now and then they come into the kitchen and joke with the personnel. Sometimes, when they earn a lot of money outside, the hostesses even treat them to something.

Okay, as he describes it, the job doesn't seem bad. He is paid well.

March 24 — Uncle Salim has been ill more than four days. At first it seemed he just had a cold, but he's been running a fever for three days now. Neither tea nor cold compresses helped, so my parents went for the doctor. After speaking with him, my father telephoned Salim's daughter in Aleppo. His son lives in America and cannot be reached.

I have never seen my father so sad. Every day when he returns from the bakery, even before he eats, he goes to see Uncle Salim and strokes his hand over and over again. Uncle Salim wants me to stay with him. I sit by his bedside until he falls asleep. My God, how small he has become, as if he'd shriveled up inside his own skin.

March 26 — Uncle Salim's daughter has arrived. I hadn't seen her in ten years. She and her father never got along. Now she is very concerned and extremely kind to him. But Uncle Salim does not treat her in a particularly friendly way. Time and again he asks her why she is here. She ought to go home to her stupid husband.

She came down to our place and wept bitter tears because her father had never forgiven her for running off with the son of his enemy. I don't understand this, and when Uncle Salim is well again, I will ask him about it. But my mother did not want to wait that long. She went down to his place and talked to him, and after a while she called for me and his daughter, then hurried into the kitchen. We ran downstairs; the old scoundrel sat bolt upright in his bed, laughing. "Come here!" he cried to his daughter. "Mrs. Hanne's words were like a cold shower. Come, let me give you a hug."

The woman sobbed on Uncle Salim's shoulder, and he kissed her on the forehead. I sat there speechless while she told him about all the things her husband had sent along and how the children (she has three) were doing. When my mother came with coffee and saw the two of them, she exclaimed, "Now things are right; anger be damned in its grave!" We all laughed.

March 28 — For three days he improved. His daughter was about to leave, but today Uncle Salim suddenly lost consciousness. In despair I ran to the doctor. (For a week I haven't been working; I explained to my boss that I did not want to leave Uncle Salim. He was very nice and said I should stay with my old friend until he recovered.) The doctor said Uncle Salim was in a very bad way. And there's nothing to be done. His heart has become too weak. Damn! I would gladly give him a part of mine.

April 5 — A coup! At dawn there was a clattering of rifles. Fighter planes thundered and swooped over the houses. For a long time the radio was silent. It was nearly noon when the agitated voice of an announcer delivered the first communiqué. The government has been toppled, because it—what else could it be?—had become corrupt and treacherous. The speaker threatened to exterminate each and every opponent of the new revolution. In the coming days a curfew would be imposed, twenty hours a day. Civilians could go out between the hours of noon and four. My father said that the new government still wasn't fully in control. It certainly sounds that way.

Uncle Salim groans lightly and is feverish. I have given his daughter my bed and have been sleeping with Leila for three days. (The monster continually lies diagonally across the bed and thrashes all night long.) Every morning my mother lights a candle for the Virgin Mary so that she will protect Uncle Salim.

April 6 — The curfew is still on; despite the danger, today I sneaked over to Habib's. He, too, senses that those in power are not yet firmly in the saddle. The air force and the navy are against them, and it gets worse from one coup to another, because each time weapons play a bigger part. It's enough that the air force is holding out. The fight for the capital might last days or weeks. Jet fighters fly over Damascus but don't drop any bombs. Damascus is firmly in the hands of the new rebels, while the northern part of the country refuses to capitulate, and the roads are blocked off.

The streets were as if swept clean when I returned. I learned from Habib that the soldiers, who have grown hysterical, shoot at anyone they see on the street. I was very careful, always walking just a few steps and then standing a while in the entrance to a house or in a side alley to observe whether a patrol was nearby.

Was my mother ever angry when I came home! She didn't want to talk to me until I promised never to do it again. And she was right. It was foolish.

Uncle Salim slept peacefully. His daughter was somewhat relieved because he woke up in the afternoon. He ate and had some tea, laughed, and asked for me.

My father sat in his room, listening to the radio in the dark. When I came in, he whispered, "They are still fighting. The navy has recognized the new regime, but the air force has nearly destroyed the radio station and the presidential palace. Aleppo resists, and the panzers are rolling northward. God protect the women and children!"

Monday, April 8 — Yesterday was the saddest day of my life. Uncle Salim, that brave and noble man, died.

What a loss for us all! My best friend is gone. He was always there for me, always stood up for me against all the adults. If I happened to play a mean or dirty trick, Uncle Salim could be very harsh with me. But he never humiliated me in front of others, as my father and schoolteachers did. No, he would take me aside, furious, and gently explain what a louse I was.

All the neighbors, grown-ups and children alike, wept, and the whole house was full of people.

He died in the night, without a sound, and left us forever. His small room is filled with flowers from his friends. My father closed the bakery and made bitter coffee—as is customary on such occasions—for all who came to offer condolences. Together with some other men, he fetched a simple casket, although going out is still prohibited. My mother helped wash Uncle Salim, all the while returning to the courtyard, where she sat down in a corner and wept. Nadia and her mother were here all day. Only her father, the miserable pig, stayed away, even though he just sat at home. Nadia fearlessly stroked my hair and held my hand because I was in a rather bad way.

Even as he entered, the priest admonished everyone to remain level-headed. A funeral procession would be dangerous, and thus he would see to getting a permit for a car in which he and the daughter of the deceased could be taken to the cemetery. Never in his whole life had my father screamed at a priest, but yesterday he was mad as hell. I was really proud of him. He shrieked that the church was no longer serving the poor but only those who drive a Mercedes. Jesus always stood up to those who abused him, but the church obeyed the orders of the most asinine officer.

"Uncle Salim," my father cried out into the dumbstruck congregation, "was not a criminal to be smuggled to the cemetery under the cover of night and fog. He was a noble man, and the funeral procession should show this!"

Men and women both supported him and decided to ignore the curfew. The priest grew pale and wanted to slip away. He said he had a baptism to perform and that he would send a deputy.

"You're staying right here," Uncle Salim's daughter

commanded, grabbing hold of the man of the cloth when he sought to get by the silent men. "If the men won't keep you here, then I will. He is my father!" she cried, and the priest stayed.

The women elected, contrary to prescribed custom, not to remain in the kitchen but to go along to the cemetery. None of them wanted to leave the men alone in their distress.

Our street had never seen the likes of this procession. Hundreds of people accompanied Uncle Salim's casket, which was borne by six men. Over two hundred women ran ahead of it; this too was something that had never been done. I walked, with Mahmud and Habib, directly behind it in the midst of the crowd. When the pallbearers reached the main road, they turned around three times in a circle so Uncle Salim could take leave of his little street; then the procession advanced into the nearby church. It was crammed full. I stayed outside with Habib, but Mahmud wanted to stand with his father right beside the coffin. Josef came late and quietly joined us. The priest gave a good speech.

From the church the funeral procession took the broad street to the East Gate of Damascus, then turned right, toward the cemetery; after a hundred paces, it suddenly came to a halt. I couldn't see anything; I just heard shrieks. We knew something had happened and ran to the front. I seized the knife in my pocket; Mahmud already had his out. A jeep blocked the street, and four soldiers aimed their machine guns at the women. But the women would not stop. They cursed out loud, and Uncle Salim's daughter tore open her black blouse and cried, "Let the procession go, and shoot me!" She forged ahead, and the other women grabbed stones from the side of the road and advanced on the retreating military officers.

When a woman cried out, "We are your sisters and mothers!" I saw a few soldiers look down at the ground. The officer in the jeep gave the command for retreat, and the vehicle sped away. I looked back and was surprised to see that Habib stood behind me with a pistol in his hand. He put its safety back on and stashed the gun in his jacket. Never in my life would I have thought that Habib owned a pistol, though I knew my father and two neighbors had taken their weapons along. I'd heard them discussing it in the stairwell. But it was the brave women who drove off the soldiers with stones.

At the graveside, Habib made a moving speech in a sad voice, speaking of the wisdom of the deceased and weeping just as the other men and women were.

P.S.: Exactly as Uncle Salim wished, I placed the marble, the key to his coach, and the dried root beside him in the casket. The priest regarded this as superstitious, but when he learned it was the request of the deceased, he agreed. All I kept was the gold coin. I will fulfill the wish of the robber and of Uncle Salim.

April 11 — Since yesterday life has returned to normal. I'm back at work. Panzer tanks are everywhere. The radio station has been destroyed, and many buildings in the New City bear the scars of battle. Uncle Salim goes on living in me, and as long as I'm alive, he will remain there.

About ten years ago his wife died. Roughly a month later, I visited him. I was seven years old at the time and already a fast friend of the old coachman. When I got there, I saw how he set the table for breakfast: two plates, two cups, two knives, and two spoons. I brought to his attention the fact that his wife had died. He smiled and said, "To you, my friend, to you she is dead. In me she is still alive and will remain so as long as I breathe."

My mother probably won't set a place for Uncle Salim next Sunday, but as long as I breathe, he will still be alive within me.

April 14 — Our silly neighbor Afifa has frightened her five-year-old daughter, and now she's bemoaning the consequences. Little Hala asked her mother why Uncle Salim died, and she answered, "Because he was old."

"But all of you are old; why aren't you dying?" the curious daughter asked.

Afifa was in a tight spot and could find no better excuse than "Uncle Salim forgot how to breathe while he was sleeping."

Now the poor child cries before going to bed because she's afraid of forgetting how to breathe. Or else she wakes up scared every night, struggling for air. And Afifa, this stupid cow? She complains that the girl has no sense of humor.

April 21 — The days go by, and yet I cannot get Uncle Salim out of my thoughts. I miss him terribly. A student moved into his little room. Sometimes when I go downstairs and hear a noise, for a few seconds I think about looking in on Uncle Salim. Funny, although I know he is dead, this happens to me repeatedly. We miss his laughter in the courtyard. No one could laugh as childishly and gaily as he.

Today I know that he was mistaken about something. "Death," he said one day, "is a long sleep." No, death is a final step. It leads somewhere, from which there is no coming back. Uncle Salim may well live on in the trees, flowers, and thistles; every kind of vegetation takes a part of him out of the earth and passes it all on: The trees—shadow and security; the flowers—fragrance and color; and the thistles—barbs and resistance. But no being on earth can make a living mixture out of all that is Uncle Salim.

No, I have lost my best friend for good. I feel lonesome. I love Mahmud and Nadia. I have great respect for Habib. But Uncle's place remains empty.

May 4 — Mahmud is now content at his job. He's no longer in the kitchen; he's serving guests in the nightclub. He doesn't make much in tips, but he gets to cheat a few rich drunks who have oodles of money.

All the women in the club are blondes. Half of them come from Europe; the other half bleach their hair because men who come to the club like to look at blondes. They dance practically naked in front of these guys who gawk at and drink with them. Of course, when the women order drinks, they demand the most expensive ones, since they get a percentage.

The owner also has them strip before certain powerful or super-rich guests. The women may be very pretty, but they drink a lot and are desperately unhappy.

May 7 — Once again Nadia's father serves a new government, hunting those formerly in power, since a few of them escaped the first wave of arrests. What a filthy pig! Nadia has nothing but contempt for him.

When I talked about Uncle Salim again today, she said something really lovely: "No one can replace a friend, but I will keep your friend's faith so that your loss will grow smaller."

I love her.

May 11 — We are preparing the fifth issue of the paper. Habib is writing an article about the Syrian coup; I, a story about friendship, which I'm dedicating to U.(ncle) S.(alim). I cannot reveal his name. Mahmud's seven questions are better than ever. They are about double standards, death, and the coup. The funniest one goes "Not only are bread and milk nowhere to be found, Oriental dancers have died out as well. In nightclubs American women wiggle and wobble before our eyes. Do you know where all these lost things have gone? Ask the revolutionary government!"

May 15 — Today Habib went to the café where authors and journalists meet and tell one another what they've heard. He declined an offer to work for the official government newspaper. He's living well enough off the translations. The book about Arsène Lupin has come out; he gave me a signed copy.

Nadia came to Habib's apartment for two hours. I showed her the newspaper strips (issues 3 and 4), and for the first time she believed me. She took me in her arms and kissed me for a long time.

She showed me how fast she can type. You can scarcely see her fingers. She learned how to do this in school.

May 21 — Today my father told me that the apprentice who took my place has left the bakery, preferring to become a smuggler. His village lies on the Lebanese border, and by smuggling, one can either quickly become very rich or else land in jail. Before he left, he trained a new boy. My father has slowly renovated the bakery, and things are going better for him. I notice this when we eat. Never before have we had so much meat on the table as in these last months. Immediately my thoughts returned to the boy who replaced me, who wanted to be an actor. He was talented, but he didn't have as good a friend as Uncle Salim.

June 2 — Issue 5 is finished! We ran off more than two thousand strips. It was an awful lot of work, but the edition is great. In very simple language Habib exposed the lies of the thirty-four rebels who have ruled Syria until now.

June 7 — We sent up five balloons with about three hundred strips, which sailed down wonderfully in the wind.

June 9 — The operation in the Umayyad Mosque was somewhat dangerous, but we were able to distribute the strips in four additional churches and in ten smaller mosques.

Habib is nearly done with the second crime novel about Arsène Lupin. He is very satisfied with himself, smokes less, and has gained some weight. Mariam loves him to distraction, but I don't think he loves her equally. He's still always thinking about his wife. Can one person love several people? I think one could love the first one intensely, the second mildly, the third . . . yes, like all the colors of the rainbow. How right the madman was.

June 13 — Mahmud is really earning a lot of money. He saves some and gives most of it to his parents. His mother is overjoyed and is dressing better and better.

Today he remarked that a few generals are regular guests for the special performance. They drink like drains and behave like pigs; even the chairs could sag in shame. He hears them talk about what they have done and boast about all the people they know.

"Wouldn't it be good to bring all their gabble to light?" I asked.

"Certainly!" Mahmud answered.

June 26 — Damn it! A catastrophe! Habib got caught!!!

I went to visit him, and from far off I saw the police cars. Two armed soldiers guarded the entrance door. I stood some distance away with many neighbors and a few curious bystanders. Again and again police officers from a special division came out of the house carrying cartons and putting them in the cars. Mariam stood on the balcony. She saw me and shook her head. Her face was dead white.

I waited until the cars drove away, then I sneaked over to her place. She fell crying into my arms and whispered, "What will I do without him? They said he was a traitor and that he got money from abroad in order to destroy the state. My poor Habib!" She sobbed in despair.

Mariam already knew we were making the paper, but she didn't say a word when friends and acquaintances of Habib's asked questions. I took her into her bedroom, where she cowered like a small child, weeping on the bed. I crept upstairs and opened the door to Habib's apartment with my key. It looked as if a pack of wolves had stormed the place. The closet was smashed up, and the photo of Habib's wife lay in tatters. Nothing in the apartment was as it had been. Tea, salt, sugar, and coffee were strewn all over the floor; dishes were broken to bits. They had taken all the books, the typewriter, the mimeograph machine, even his laundry.

Mahmud was terribly shocked when he learned about it. There is no trace of fear in him personally, but he's terrified for Habib's life. They will beat him to death or drive him mad and then put him in an insane asylum.

June 29 — I discussed it with Mahmud. He thought it was now time to give up the gold coin for Habib, that we should get a lawyer with it. But we can't find one! They gave Mahmud evasive answers as to why they could not take the case, just as they gave me. One alone was honorable, explaining that the defense of political prisoners is prohibited in Syria. Nadia confirmed this. Her boss, that show-off who is always bragging about how many judges have passed through his hands, looked at Nadia with suspicion when she inquired. He brusquely advised her that if she wanted to go on working for him, she had better get back to typing letters and refrain from speaking of political cases in his offices.

Evidently a flyer is more dangerous than a murder in this country.

July 1 — Tonight BBC London brought word of the arrest. They must have gotten it from the French paper *Le Monde*. Thanks to his intrepid journalistic activity, Habib was arrested.

July 4 — Not until the ninth day did the government newspaper report that a madman by the name of Habib had for a while published a silly newspaper and now was in treatment.

My boss is extremely peculiar. He scoffed at Habib for having been so idiotic as to have set himself against the entire bureaucracy alone. The gutless dog, I could have spit in his face.

July 10 — Yesterday we sat together for a long time, pondering what we could do. We have to get Habib out. But how?

Mahmud suggested that we abduct a general from the nightclub and demand Habib's release in exchange. Not a bad idea, I thought, and tomorrow I'll go there and look the club over. Mahmud can offer me a free drink.

My boss found out from some big shot that Habib is beyond help. The guy claimed he could spring any pimp, hashish smuggler, or knifer, but he wouldn't touch a political prisoner; he didn't want to get his fingers burned.

The Journalists' Association also rebuffed my boss. "Habib," they said, "is sick and irresponsible."

July 11 — Nadia thinks our idea stinks. She bawled us out for being so stupid and naive as to believe any one general could be so important. She laughed scornfully and yelled at me, "Who knows, maybe you'll get a medal for having spared the government the trouble of getting rid of a general it wanted to dispose of and didn't know how to. But Habib won't come out of it alive."

July 12 — Last night I went to the club. I told my mother, and she's supposed to invent something if my old man asks about me. But I promised her I would neither spend money nor have anything to do with the women there. I would only visit Mahmud and see how he does his job.

The club is sheer madness! One can scarcely believe anything like it exists in Damascus. Outside, the women we come in contact with refuse even a kiss, and inside they sit and indulge in the wildest Parisian life.

Mahmud pointed out the minister of justice and then the air force general who took so long to accept the government. These guys don't look the least bit frightening. The general was a rather small and emaciated man of fifty, dressed in civilian attire. I could have taken him for a cattle dealer or the keeper of a small shop. Uniforms really do make all the difference!

A somewhat fat blonde performed an Oriental dance. That really was something to see! It simply couldn't be called dancing; it was nothing but a waggling of fat. Still, the men cheered each time she bent over and showed her breasts. After two drinks, the general was drunk and ostentatiously spoke English—but so badly that I commiserated with his English teacher. The guy had no idea what he was saying; he translated his Arabic exclamations into English word for word. What is lovely in Arabic is macabre in a verbatim translation.

"Oh, my eyeapple," he cooed enthusiastically. "You bury me, you sweet bee," he called to the dancer while rolling his eyes.

Nadia is right. Any government would love to be rid of such an idiot. They can easily replace him with a similar dope. This evening I will talk to Mahmud and Nadia again.

July 13 — Today I was in the cemetery, at Uncle Salim's modest grave. It does not distinguish itself from the earth that bore him and to which he has returned. I set five red roses on it.

My sadness for Habib is nearly choking me, but I want to live and laugh. I don't want to give up hope. My old friend Salim taught me this.

"Everything grows," he said to me one day. "Everything grows, except for catastrophe. It is largest at birth, and then it shrinks from day to day."

July 14 — We spoke for a long time together. Mahmud also became pensive when Nadia asked him, "What do you think Habib would most like to do now?"

"Make another newspaper," we whispered as if with one voice.

"Exactly, the newspaper. These murderers ought to know that if they kill Habib, many Habibs will spring up in his place."

Nadia wants to collaborate. She wants to report on the women of Damascus; Mahmud is writing about some of the secrets of the last coup. I am writing an article about Habib, the bravest journalist in Syria; Mahmud and Nadia decided this, since I am the one who knows Habib best.

Mahmud has spent two hundred pounds of his savings on a mimeograph machine and a typewriter. And I contributed a hundred for paper, ink, and balloons.

It took some time to find a hideout where we could set up our "press." Here Mariam was a great help. She has an old friend who rents rooms to students. Because the term is over, an attic room has been vacant for a week. It's very cheap, and young people are constantly going in and out of the house it's in. The woman who owns the house lives a couple of blocks away in a nice neighborhood; she doesn't care who her tenants are. The main thing is that the rent be paid each month in advance. Mariam is taking care of this for us and for Habib.

Tomorrow I'll go with her to visit the woman and pick up the key. I'll pretend to be a freshly baked student and that my father is a rich farmer up north. Three months' rent will convince her.

Habib needs the newspaper. We will show the military just how many Habibs the imprisoned journalist has brought into the world.

A Hand Full of Stars

The *Hand* is the hand of Uncle Salim, always there to guide the narrator; in the saddest moments, it points the way out of despair. Like the stars that illuminate the dark night sky, the *Stars* in the hand stand for hope.

—R. S.

DATE DUE	
GAYLORD	PRINTED IN U.S.A.